THE HOM
Palli

SARAT CHANDRA CHATTERJEE

THE HOMECOMING
Palli Samaj

Translated by

PRASENJIT MUKHERJEE

Rupa & Co

Translation Prasenjit mukherjee 1988

First in Rupa Paperback 1989
Second impression 2001

Published by
Rupa & Co.
7/16, Ansari Road, Daryaganj,
New Delhi 110 002

Offices at:
15 Bankim Chatterjee Street, Calcutta 700 073
135 South Malaka, Allahabad 211 001
PG Solanki Path, Lamington Road, Mumbai 400 007
36, Kutty Street, Nungambakkam, Chennai 600 034
Surya Shree, B-6, New 66, Shankara Park,
Basavangudi, Bangalore 560 004
3-5-612, Himayat Nagar, Hyderabad 500 029

Printed in India by
Gopsons Papers Ltd.
A-14 Sector 60
Noida 201 301

Rs 150

TO MY FATHER

INTRODUCTION

Saratchandra Chattopadhyay (or Chatterjee) was born
on 15 September, 1876, at Devanandapur, a village in
the district of Hooghly in West Bengal, not very far from
Calcutta. He was the eldest son of Motilal Chattopadhyay and Bhubanmohini, daughter of Kedarnath
Ganguly of Bhagalpur in Bihar. According to the preva-
lent custom, Motilal, a Brahmin of the highest class,
married at an early age, when he was only fourteen or
fifteen. He completed his education in his father-in-
law's house at Bhagalpur and passed the university
entrance examination. However, except for a brief period of about two years (1884-1886), when Motilal
served at Dehri-on-Sone, he remained mostly unemployed and had to pass his days in poverty. Bhubanmohini used to stay most of the time with her parents at
Bhagalpur, along with her children and sometimes with
her husband also.

Saratchandra received his early education at Devanandapur and Bhagalpur. He passed the entrance examination at Bhagalpur, in December, 1894. He then
joined the First Arts class in T.N. Jubilee College.
Unfortunately, his mother died the next year.
Bhubanmohini's death was nothing short of a disaster
for the family. After his wife's death, Motilal set up a
separate establishment at Bhagalpur with his children.
His Devanandapur house was sold in repayment of a
loan. Next year, when the time came for his university
examination, Saratchandra was unable to appear at the
examination. This was the end of his formal education.

For some time in 1899, Saratchandra served under

the Boneli Raj Estate in connection with their land-settlement work in Santhal Parganas. He had to live in a tent and cook his own food. The landowner's son used to visit the camp from time to time. During his visit music and dance soirees were held. This was a new experience for Saratchandra. When this work was over, he returned to Bhagalpur.

Except for this short period, Saratchandra had to remain unemployed for a number of years. He utilized his time in literary pursuits and in intensive study of Bengali, English and continental literature in the library of his friend and neighbour, Bibhutibhushan Bhatta. During this time he also acquired some proficiency in music and interested himself in drama and took part in the theatrical performances organized by the Adampur Amateur Dramatic Club.

One day, towards the end of 1901, aggrieved at his father's rebuke, Saratchandra left his house and went away in the company of a band of Hindu mendicants. In course of his wanderings he came to Muzaffarpur, where he received the news of his father's sudden death, in the middle of 1902, and hastened to Bhagalpur.

When his father's funeral was over, Saratchandra went to Calcutta in search of a job. Having failed to secure a suitable job there, Saratchandra left in January 1903 for Burma, where Aghorenath Banerjee, husband of one of his mother's cousins, was a successful lawyer. There he served temporarily, first at Pegu and then at Rangoon, and at last received a permanent appointment in the office of the Deputy Accountant-General, Rangoon. He served there till May 1916, when he returned to India, to devote himself exclusively to literature.

In 1921, Saratchandra joined the freedom struggle and came in close contact with Chittaranjan Das and Subhas Chandra Bose. He worked as Chairman of the Howrah District Congress Committee for a number of years and was also a member of the Bengal Provincial Congress Committee and the All-India Congress Committee. When his novel *Pather Dabi*, dealing with the revolutionary movement, was published in 1926, it was proscribed by the British Government.

In 1923, the University of Calcutta awarded the Jagattarini Gold Medal to Saratchandra. The first recipient of this award was Rabindranath Tagore, in 1921. In July 1936, the honorary degree of Doctor of Literature was conferred upon Saratchandra by the University of Dacca.

Saratchandra died on 16 January, 1938, at the age of sixty-two.

II

Saratchandra has given us the following account of his literary career:

'My childhood and youth were passed in great poverty. I received almost no education for want of means. From my father I inherited nothing except, as I believe, his restless spirit and keen interest in literature. The first made me a tramp and sent me out tramping the whole of India quite early, and the second made me a dreamer all my life. Father was a great scholar and he tried his hand on stories and novels, dramas and poems; in short, every branch of literature, but never could finish anything. I have not his work now; somehow, it got lost; but I remember poring over these incomplete MSS over and over again in my childhood, and many a night I kept awake regretting their incompleteness and thinking what might have been their conclusion, if finished. Probably this led to my writing short stories when I was barely seventeen. But I soon gave up the habit as useless, and almost forgot in the long years that followed that I could even write a sentence in my boyhood. A mere accident made me start again, after the lapse of about eighteen years. Some of my old acquaintances started a little magazine, but no one of note would condescend to contribute to it, as it was so small and insignificant. When almost hopeless, some of them suddenly remembered me, and after much persuasion they succeeded in extracting from me a promise to write for it. This was in the year 1913. I promised most unwillingly – perhaps only to put them off till I had returned to Rangoon and could forget all about it. But the sheer volume and force of their letters and telegrams compelled me at last to think seriously about writing again. I sent them a short story, for their magazine *Jamuna*. This became at once extremely popular and made me famous in one day. Since then I have been writing regularly. In Bengal perhaps I am the only fortunate writer who has not had to struggle.'

Saratchandra started writing stories at Devanandapur, when he was only seventeen. It was during this time that he made the first drafts of *Kashinath* and *Korelgram* (later renamed *Chhabi*). Later when Saratchandra moved to Bhagalpur, he established a literary club there and began to write for its handwritten monthly magazine *Chhaya*. Saratchandra wrote *Bojha, Abhiman* (after Mrs. Henry Wood's novel *East Lynne*), *Basha, Anupamar Prem, Sukumarer Balya Katha, Pashan* (after Mary Correli's *Mighty Atom*), *Bar Didi, Chandranath, Haricharan, Devdas, Balya Smriti* and *Shubhada*, etc., during this period.
    Saratchandra's first published literary work was a short story named 'Mandir' which won the first prize in the 'Kuntalin' literary competition in 1903. In 1907 *Bar Didi*, a novel, appeared serially in the monthly magazine *Bharati*. The first two instalments did not bear the author's name. At that time many took it to be a new story by Rabindranath, published anonymously. This shows the impact which *Bar Bidi* had on the public

x

mind. Although the new author was a complete stranger in the literary circles of Bengal, *Bar Bidi* caused a furore and heralded the emergence of a new star in the firmament of Bengali literature. It proved to be a turning point in Saratchandra's life.

When Saratchandra visited Calcutta in the latter part of 1912, he was persuaded by his maternal uncle, Upendranath Ganguly, to write for the newly-established monthly magazine *Jamuna*. He agreed and on return to Rangoon, resumed his literary work and a number of novels came out in quick succession. When *Ramer Sumati, Bindur Chele* and *Patha Nirdesh,* and later a portion of *Charitraheen* appeared on the pages of *Jamuna*, they firmly established Saratchandra's reputation and made him famous almost overnight as a great novelist.

Later, on receipt of a decent offer from the publishers of the monthly magazine *Bharatvarsha*, Saratchandra came to India, in May 1916, to devote himself exclusively to literature. The decade that followed saw the fullest development of his genius and was the most fruitful. During this period appeared, among others, *Srikanta, Charitraheen, Datta, Grihadaha, Dena Paona* and *Pather Dabi.*

When *Charitraheen, Srikanta, Palli Samaj* and later *Grihadaha* were published, Saratchandra had to face bitter and hostile criticism from the conservative section of the society. *Charitraheen* especially, with its depiction of extra-marital love, provoked the bitterest attacks and for some time Saratchandra became a controversial figure in Bengali literature. He was the first novelist who had the breadth of vision, courage of conviction, liberality of mind, and human sympathy to depict in literature the lives of fallen women.

Saratchandra firmly believed that a woman's steadfast and unswerving love for her lover, even though not her husband, was in no way less honourable than the so-called chastity of married women, many of whom had never experienced real love for their husbands. He said:

'Man's idea of a woman's chastity has not always remained the same. It was not so in the past, and it may not be so in future also. If steadfast love, as distinct from chastity, has no place even in literature, will it be a true image of life ? I do not belittle the value of chastity, but consider that it is a superstition to make a fetish of it and treat it as the be-all and end-all of a woman's life.'

Later, the opposition subsided and in course of time it died. Subsequent generations of young novelists have followed the tradition that Saratchandra set, and have done a lot towards extending the area and range of the Bengali novel.

III

Palli Samaj was first published in the monthly magazine *Bharatvarsha*, in its issues for the months of Aswin (September-October, 1915) and Agrahayan (November-December, 1915). It was published in a book form on 15 January, 1916.

The story is laid in a village near Tarakeshwar, in the district of Hooghly in West Bengal; in the area where the author's own birth-place, Devanandapur, is situated. The time is apparently towards the end of the nineteenth century, when the village life was dominated by superstitious social conventions and caste prejudices, and social power was wielded by the richer section of the society, namely, the landowners and the moneylenders, and, to a lesser extent, by the Brahmins. The low-born and the poor were completely at the mercy of the leaders of the society who dealt with them in any way they liked. The rigid social structure in the village had reduced their very existence to an almost subhuman level.

The novel deals with the efforts of Ramesh, a young Roorkee-trained engineer, to bring about some change in the caste-ridden village and to elevate the villagers to a better level of existence. The novel deals in depth with the malady that infects the village, strives to unearth its causes and offers some remedy. In the end we find that Ramesh's efforts have been rewarded, the opposition has died and the scene is set for a better future.

A complication arises in the plot when Ramesh and his boyhood friend Rama, now a young widow, fall in love. As a widow in the tradition-bound Hindu society, Rama could not marry Ramesh, which should otherwise have been the fruition of their love. The brief scene at Tarakeshwar shows how Ramesh and Rama would have acted normally without the spectre of social ostracism looming large before them. Rama's departure for Benares at the end of the novel was the stratagem adopted by the author to solve the tangle, but it shattered the lives of the two lovers. This is what Saratchandra himself said:

'I have a novelette named *Palli Samaj*. In it the heroine Rama, a young Hindu widow, fell in love with her childhood friend Ramesh. I had to face bitter criticism on this account. One eminent critic even went to the length of complaining that if such immorality in literature was tolerated by the society, there would not be any widow left in any village in future ! A matter for grave anxiety indeed ! It is not for me to say whether this would lead the Hindu society to hell. I can only say that at no time and in no society men like Ramesh and women like Rama were in plenty. It is not difficult to imagine the glory of the lives of these two lovers happily united in wedlock. But there was no place for such a union in the Hindu society of the day. As a result, the lives of these two noble souls became infructuous. Whether this was a loss or a gain for the Hindu society is not for me to say:

xiii

that is for the society to consider. If I have been able to convey the message of their pathetic story to the closed hearts of the Hindu society, my work is done. Like the futility of Rama's life, this novelette may fail in achieving its object, but I have no doubt in my mind that in the years to come, a more enlightened society will take a different view.'

Critics are divided on the question of the theme of the novel. Some have held that the love story of Ramesh and Rama is the main theme and the village community is only the background or the setting for the story; it does not act as an independent entity or force; while others are of the opinion that the portrayal of the miserable condition of the village, protest against the oppression and tyranny of the village community and the village development work is the real theme of the novel. They hold that the love story, which flows like an undercurrent throughout the novel, is only a secondary theme – a subplot used by the author to expose the heartless and unscrupulous character of the society. Such dispute, however, does not seem to be of any practical significance. Both the themes are interrelated and each forms an integral part of the other.

The novel moves along primarily on two levels : the social level and the personal level. In the former, the note is one of optimism and exultation at the awareness of a new life that at last comes to the people. But on the personal level, it ends in a tragedy. The tragedy is not the result of any personal failings on the part of Rama and Ramesh; it is the outcome of a rigid stance adopted by a moribund society unwilling to move with the changing times. The social life in the village changes for the better and shows a definite awareness, but it is not yet prepared to accept the revolutionary change in outlook so as to allow the two lovers to live a contented life. However, it is Rama's and Ramesh's understanding of each other at the end of the novel that takes away the bitterness.

The novel, which stretches over a period of a year and a half, traces the development of the chain of events that begins with Ramesh's arrival at Kuanpur. As the action in the novel is set in motion, the tension in the relationship between Rama and Ramesh mounts, abetted by the acts of intervention on the part of the other figures. The novel is clearly divided into two parts, the first nine chapters showing the gradual growth of Rama's and Ramesh's love for each other, the subsequent nine chapters showing the events that obstruct the smooth flow of their love and lead to Bishweshwari's and Rama's departure for Benares. Since Rama was a widow and her relationship with Ramesh was unacceptable to the society, an equilibrium could not be reached; the novel had to end in a moral resolution rather than on the level of physical love.

The intervening chapter between the two parts, namely, the tenth, which describes Rama and Ramesh's meeting at Tarakeshwar, occupies the central position in the love story. This is the crisis of the action, the Aristotelian middle of the plot. Everything thus far has moved towards it, but now everything moves towards a different end, determined by it. The climax is reached in the very last chapter with the departure of Bishweshwari and Rama. Rama's departure brings to a tragic end her relations with Ramesh.

Rama and Ramesh thus turn out to be tragic characters, in the sense that because of some external agency, which is more powerful than they, their love cannot be fulfilled. Yet the tragic reconciliation consists in the fact that they get an insight into the love each has for the other if not on the level of action, at least on the spiritual plane. They achieve sublimation in their decision to live within the bounds of the society into which they were born. They decide to resign themselves to their fate stoically and in this context society assumes the dimension of Fate in Greek tragedy.

The novel begins with an arrival and ends with a departure. Between these two incidents is encompassed a whole world of rural life. Though the scene of the action is limited to Kuanpur and adjoining Pirpur, with only a brief interlude at Tarakeshwar, yet a host of characters, representing all walks of life in a village, fill the pages of the novel. Their purpose is to give relief and provide the background – the society out of which Rama and Ramesh emerge into focus and into which they melt after the story is over. Unlike the rustic characters of Hardy who exist only in the poetic level contributing little to the development of action in the novel, the rustic characters in this dramatic novel of Saratchandra have a direct bearing on the action and consequently on the total meaning of the novel. Ultimately they provide full-bloodedness to the representation of reality.

Conflict in *Palli Samaj* is viewed on three levels : Ramesh's conflict with the villagers and Beni is on the physical level; his tension with Rama that arises from his feelings of attraction-repulsion towards her belongs to the emotional level; while his conflict within himself belongs to an intellectual level. The last chapter, however, resolves all the conflicts and places Ramesh where he rightly belongs, in the midst of all the villagers.

As a novelist, Saratchandra is not interested in physical confrontations in themselves as much as in the effect such confrontations may have on human relationship and character. All the physical confrontations that take place in this novel are carefully kept off-stage; we come to know of them only through reports. The only physical confrontation that Saratchandra directly deals with is the so-called 'assault' on Bhairab by Ramesh. Even in this case Saratchandra has chosen to depict the incident because it has a direct bearing not only on the subsequent action but also on the later development of the characters. The human significance arising from the interaction of different characters gives the novelist a greater chance to build up characters elaborately. The conspicuous avoidance of physical actions in his novels, as in Greek drama, marks out Saratchandra as a psychological novelist rather than a novelist of plot and action.

The dramatic nature of the novel and the author's excessive involvement with the social aspect of life both leave their marks on the language of *Palli Samaj*. The chief characteristic of the language is its laconic brevity. Except for symbolic representations of natural phenomena now and then, such as the cloudy sky, frosty moonlight, the clear moonlight nights and the morning sun rising in the eastern sky, *Palli Samaj* seems bereft of such natural description that *Srikanta* abounds in. Moreover, whatever description is used, is used with a view to highlighting different facets of a character's personality; and elements which do not have any bearing on the progression of action are sedulously avoided. This attitude of the novelist affects the language adversely. The language is at times sparse, having neither the sweep nor the flow of Saratchandra's more imaginative writings like *Srikanta*.

The dialogues, however, are brilliant and remind one of the glittering word-play which characterized Saratchandra's best work. A dramatic novel depends to a great extent on the force and power of its dialogues. Likewise the dramatic element in *Palli Samaj* is largely brought in by its racy colloquial dialogue. It is interesting to note that only in respect of his dialogues does Saratchandra use colloquial speech. The rest of the book is written in 'literary' Bengali.

The dialogues in *Palli Samaj* have a wide range and are instrumental in showing the basic traits of the characters. The language that Beni uses is different from that of Ramesh, as the language used by Bishweshwari is different from that used by Rama's aunt. The language plays an important role in revealing the psychological make-up of each of the characters. Beni's twisted and tortuous language reveals his own scheming mind. Govinda Ganguly's insincerity, hypocrisy and fawning nature come out clearly in his language. The language in *Palli Samaj* contributes largely to the understanding of characters.

The main characters, Rama and Ramesh, are however remarkable in their reticence. Throughout the novel Rama does not speak a single word to indicate her love for Ramesh, but a tension is created by her very silence. Though Rama and Ramesh are extremely formal in their talk and manner, their affection for each other is present like a palpable force charging the atmosphere around them. In such a tension words are hardly necessary; their reticence is remarkable in its expressiveness.

Palli Samaj is a piece of social criticism. In it Saratchandra has criticized the rural Hindu society and pointed out its defects – its intolerance, its unwillingness to move with the time, its oppression, injustice, and even cruelty, its exploitation and neglect of the so-called 'low-caste' people in such lurid light that when it was published it shocked the orthodox section of the society. It was the intention of the author to give a jolt to the society to rouse it from the stupor into which it had fallen. The festering sores which were vitiating the social life and eating into its vitals were exposed by Saratchandra in order to give it the healing touch of the open air and sunshine.

Saratchandra pointed out the defects of the society, but did not always suggest remedies. As he said : 'Social reform is not my domain. My novels show the human sufferings caused by the society; they pose the problems but do not attempt to offer any solution, because I am not a social reformer. I am simply a story-teller.'

Yet he has, in fact, suggested some remedies, as in

Palli Samaj, where he has exhorted educated young men to go back to the villages and to take up village reconstruction work and to spread education among the masses. In a letter from Rangoon Saratchandra wrote: 'The remedy lies only in the spread of knowledge. These who want to work for the upliftment of the villagers should preferably be brought up and educated away from the villages so that they acquire a wider outlook. They should then come back to the villages and settle there and should mix freely with all the villagers, good and bad, so as to gain their confidence.'

At the core of *Palli Samaj* lies this idea of Saratchandra. It is interesting to note that Bishweshwari echoes the sentiments expressed by the author in this letter.

With *Palli Samaj*, the realistic novel in Bengal reached a new high. The village life with its factionalism and quarrels among the villagers, which work as divisive forces and cut at the roots of their unity; their extreme poverty, indebtedness and exploitation by the moneylenders; ravages caused by malaria; ruinous litigations; fraud and forgery; exploitation of the poor by misusing the laws of the land; police excesses; moral degradation, ignorance and illiteracy; Hindu-Muslim relations; and above all tyranny in the name of religion – the novelist has portrayed all these with great realism, making the novel almost kaleidoscopic in nature.

The social conditions in Bengal villages, as described in *Palli Samaj*, have undergone some change since the time when the book was first published in 1916, especially after the attainment of independence, the abolition of estates and the introduction of various rural upliftment schemes. To that extent the novel might have lost some of its topical interest and significance, but its basic appeal still remains as fresh as ever. Has there really been any change for the better in the character of the villagers? Has the exodus from the villages to towns since decreased? Are not thousands of

Indian villages still in as deplorable a state of neglect as the village of Kuanpur in *Palli Samaj* ? In fact, even today, seventy-two years after the publication of this novel, some of the problems that Saratchandra posed in it still await solution.

TRANSLATOR'S NOTE

Translation of a novel consists of something more than just presenting the story in another language, a new garb. It consists, in its broader perspective, in transforming one milieu into another. The translator's aim is, therefore, not only to translate a book, but also to make it live in the other language, so that the reader may acquaint himself satisfactorily with the lives of the characters reflected in the many actions that take place, the customs and rituals, and the elusive relationship of the characters with these; in fact, with their complete social ethos. The translated work can, of course, never stand on the same level with the original. The novelist's language has its roots in the tradition of the race and hence every word that the novelist writes is loaded with connotative associations which go much deeper than their contextual references. The translator can only hope to translate it as an objective viewer. Mr. T.W. Clark, in his Introduction to *Pather Panchali*, takes the example of the word *ekadashi*. Similarly, in Chapter II of *Palli Samaj,* the author writes *karma-bari.* The suggestiveness of such words is much greater than their contextual meaning, and as their grass-roots go deep into the social life and mores of the people, the translator has not only to translate the word but also to bring out the entire range of associations connected with it. Only then does it make sense to the reader.

Besides this, there is another difficulty which every translator has to face. This is the difficulty of finding English equivalents of the Indian alphabets. There is, of course, an excellent monograph published by the West

Bengal Government (Home and Political Department) on this subject. There is also Dr. Suniti Kumar Chatterji's scholarship to help the translator in his work, but neither the former nor the latter appears to solve the problem to one's complete satisfaction.

Every translator of a Bengali novel comes across certain words and phrases which cannot be translated satisfactorily into English. Giving approximate expressions to such words and phrases does not solve the problem either. Different translators have adopted different methods to overcome this difficulty. Some prefer to give the approximate English equivalent within brackets after the word which they retain in its native garb. Others give the meaning and the equivalent in the glossary at the back of the book. Lengthy glossaries have, however, the initial risk of remaining unread most of the time, and giving the equivalent within brackets often interrupts the flow of the narrative.

A compromise has, therefore, been struck by sometimes using near-equivalent English terms, and where this is not at all possible, to retain the original Bengali term, which is subsequently sought to be clarified in the glossary provided at the end of the book. The real function of the glossary is, however, more to tackle the cultural problem that crops up while presenting a whole social milieu in another language, and also to explain the social background of the novel.

Palli Samaj is a book on rustic life. It is therefore natural that the novelist should use colloquial speech throughout the novel. However, it is only the dialogues, which have been written in the colloquial style; the rest of the book is presented in 'literary' Bengali. I have attempted to reproduce, as far as possible, the speech-patterns that the novelist used in the dialogues of the rustic people, without violating the English idiom as far as practicable. I have therefore used colloquial speech throughout the book and introduced slangy expressions wherever necessary. If, in doing so, the grammatical and syntactical structure of the sentences has been altered a bit, it has been done with a view to preserving the flavour of the original and the essential spirit of the novel.

Lastly, regarding the title of the novel, though the title *Palli Samaj* when literally translated would be 'Village Community', I have chosen 'The Homecoming', since the entire action in the novel emanates from the homecoming of the hero, and the problems it creates, after the death of his father.

wherever necessary. In abridging these grammatical and syntactical structure of the sentences has been altered a bit, it has been done with a view to preserve the flavour of the original and the essential part of the novel.

Lastly, regarding the title of the novel, though the Bengali word 'People' is a better translated word for 'Village' meaning, I have chosen 'The Hero' since more the entire scene of the novel centres round the heroic saga of the hero, and the problems born arise after the end of the Hero.

xxiii

CHAPTER
1

Beni Ghoshal stepped into the inner courtyard of the Mukharji home and, seeing an elderly woman there, asked, 'Hallo Aunt, where's Rama?'

The lady was engaged in her prayers. So she did not reply, but pointed to the kitchen. Beni went up to the kitchen and, standing outside the door, said, 'Well, Rama, what've you decided about the matter?'

Rama took the sizzling pan off the oven and, looking up at Beni, said, 'About what, Dada?'

'About Tarini Uncle's funeral ceremony,' replied Beni. 'Ramesh came home yesterday. Looks like he'll perform the ceremony on a grand scale. Are you going to attend the function?'

Rama stared at Beni with her eyes wide open in utter surprise. 'How on earth could you think that I'd go to Tarini Ghoshal's house?'

Beni was a little embarrassed. 'I know, I know; whoever else may go, you never will! But I'm told that Ramesh'll go from door to door and invite every one personally—he seems to excel his father in cunning! In case he comes to invite you, what'll you say?'

'I'll say nothing —my watchman at the gate will give the answer!' retorted Rama angrily.

As soon as this extremely agreeable talk about family feud reached Aunt's ears, she brushed her prayers aside and came over. Before her niece could finish, she burst out with a sudden jerk, like a grain of puffed rice leaping out of an over-heated frying pan. 'Why the watchman?

1

Don't I know how to speak? I'll give that rascal such a good talking-to that he'll never cross the threshold of the Mukharji home again! Tarini Ghoshal's son enter our house to invite us! I've forgotten nothing, Beni-madhab. Tarini had wanted to marry this son of his to my Rama. My Jatin hadn't then been born. Tarini must've thought that thereby he'd be able to grab the entire property of Jadu Mukharji....You understand that, don't you Beni! But when he couldn't succeed, he engaged this fellow Bhairab Acharjya to employ some black magic for bringing bad luck to my Rama. Even within six months of her marriage, the poor girl became a widow. How impudent of the low-caste fellow to think of having Jadu Mukharji's daughter for his son! Well, the rascal has been rightly served in his death – he couldn't even have his cremation fire lit by his son! Damn the low-caste rogue!'

Aunt stood panting for breath as if she had just finished a bout of wrestling.

Repeated mention of the word 'low-caste' had made Beni lose colour, because Tarini Ghoshal was after all his own uncle. Rama noticed this and spoke reprovingly to her aunt, 'Why do you raise the question of caste, Aunt? Nobody has any choice in this matter. Wherever one is born, that's best for him.'

Beni smiled shamefacedly and said, 'No, Rama, Aunt's right. You're the daughter of a high-ranking Brahmin. How could we expect to have you as a daughter-in-law in our family? It was sheer impertinence on Uncle's part to make such a proposal. And as regards the black magic, there must be some truth in it. Nothing on earth was impossible for my uncle and that rascal Bhairab Acharjya. And just imagine, that fellow Bhairab has become Ramesh's adviser these days!'

'Well, Beni, that's what we knew was coming,' re-marked Aunt. 'This fellow Ramesh hasn't been to the

2

village all these ten or twelve years! Where was he all this time?'

'How do I know, Aunt?' replied Beni. 'My relations with Uncle were the same as yours. But I'm told he was in Bombay or some such place. Some say he's become a doctor, while others say, a lawyer. Yet there are people who hold that it's all bogus – he's just a drunk. They say when he arrived home, his eyes were as red as hibiscus.'

'Really? Then he mustn't be allowed to enter this house at all!'

'No, of course not !'said Beni emphatically, with a decisive shake of his head. 'Well Rama, do you remember Ramesh?'

The recounting of the story of her ill-luck had embarrassed Rama. She replied bashfully, 'Yes, I do. He isn't much older than I. Besides, we both attended the village school together. But I remember his mother's death very well. Aunty used to love me dearly.'

Aunt flared up once again and snapped, 'To hell with that love! Such love was meant just to achieve their objective! They wanted to grab you somehow.'

Beni sagely agreed with her and said, 'Is there any doubt about it, Aunt? Aunty was....' But before he could finish, Rama interrupted and said to her aunt, with apparent displeasure, 'It's no use stirring up the past.'

In spite of all her quarrels with Ramesh's father Rama still had a soft corner for his mother. This had not completely disappeared over all these years.

Beni at once agreed with Rama and said, 'Yes, yes, that's right. Aunty was indeed the daughter of a good man. My mother still sheds tears at the mention of her name.'

Noticing that the talk was taking an inconvenient turn, Beni immediately changed the subject and said, 'Well, so it's finally settled that you aren't going to attend the function. I hope you won't change your mind.'

Rama smiled. 'You know, Dada, my father used to tell me, "Don't ever keep the last traces of a fire, a debt or an enemy, my girl." So long as Tarini Ghoshal lived, he gave us no end of trouble. He even tried to send my father to jail. I haven't forgotten all that, nor shall I forget it as long as I live. After all, Ramesh is that enemy's son! Besides, it isn't at all possible for me to go. It's true my father divided his property between my brother and me, but the responsibility for preserving it intact rests entirely with me. Not to speak of us, I wouldn't even allow anyone connected with our family to attend the function.'

After a little pause she added, 'Dada, can't you so arrange that not a single Brahmin attends the function!'

Beni came closer, lowered his voice and said, 'That's exactly what I'm trying to do. So long you're there to help me, I don't care a fig for anyone else. I swear I'll drive away this Ramesh from Kuanpur; otherwise I'm not Beni Ghoshal! After that, I'll deal with Bhairab. Now that Tarini Ghoshal's dead, I'll see who can save that rascal.'

'Why, Ramesh Ghoshal will save him', said Rama. 'You can take it from me, Dada, he'll prove himself an equally formidable enemy.'

Beni came still closer, looked around, then squatted on the door frame and said, almost in a whisper, 'Rama, if you want to bend the bamboo, this is the right moment. I can tell you for certain that once it's full-grown, you won't succeed. Ramesh hasn't yet learnt the tricks of managing an estate...if we can't finish him off now, it won't be possible to do so in future. We mustn't forget that Ramesh is none other than Tarini Ghoshal's son!'

'I know that very well, Dada.'

'Of course you do. I believe God was going to make you a boy, but he slipped up somewhere and you turned out to be a girl. We all admit to ourselves that in intelligence

4

even an experienced landowner is no match for you. It's getting late. I'd better push off now. I'll be seeing you again tomorrow.' So saying Beni got up.

Rama was highly pleased with the compliments paid to her by Beni. She also got up, and was just going to make a mild protest out of modesty, when she heard, with a pang in her heart, a deep unfamiliar voice calling out from the other end of the courtyard. 'Are you in, Rani?'

In her childhood Ramesh's mother used to call her by this name. She had herself long forgotten it. Looking at Beni she found his face had turned ashen. Next moment Ramesh appeared, with unkempt hair, bare feet, and a scarf wrapped round his head. As soon as he saw Beni, he said, 'Hallo, Dada, so you're here! I've been looking for you all over the place. Do come and help with the arrangements for the ceremony. Who else is there to do it? Where's Rani?' He came and stood in front of the kitchen door.

Rama had no way of escape. She remained standing with downcast eyes. Ramesh cast a glance at her and spoke like one greatly surprised.

'Oh, my! Rani, how you've grown! I hope you're well?'

Rama stood rooted to the spot as before, unable to utter a single word. Ramesh hastily added, with a smile, 'But have you been able to recognize me? I'm your Ramesh-da.'

Rama could not still raise her eyes and look at him. But now she said in a low voice, 'Are you well?'

'Yes, I'm well. But why talk to me so formally, Rama?' Ramesh then turned to Beni and said, with a wan smile on his lips, 'I can never forget, Dada, what Rama told me when mother died; she was just a small girl then, but even at that age she wiped the tears from my eyes and consoled me. "Don't cry, Ramesh-da", she said. "I'll share my mother with you." Perhaps you don't remember that, Rani, but do you remember my mother?'

5

At this Rama felt all the more embarrassed and her head hung lower. She could not even nod her head to indicate that she still remembered her Aunty very well.

Ramesh now spoke pointedly to Rama, 'There's hardly any time left for the ceremony – just three more days. Do help me make the arrangements. I have come to your door as a destitute to seek your help. Unless you all come and help, I can do nothing.'

Aunt came and stood silently behind Ramesh. When neither Beni nor Rama gave any reply, she came round and stood in front of Ramesh and, looking up at him, said, 'You're Tarini Ghoshal's son, aren't you?'

Ramesh had not seen this Aunt before, for she came to this village after Ramesh had left. She first entered the Mukharji household on the pretext of the illness of Rama's mother and never left it again.

Ramesh stared at her, rather surprised. Aunt continued, 'Who else could be so shameless! Like father, like son! Aren't you ashamed of yourself entering into a woman's house without her permission, and creating a racket?'

Completely bewildered, Ramesh stood fixed to the spot like a statue.

'I must get going', murmured Beni, and left in a hurry.

Rama now said from inside the room, 'What's this rubbish you're talking, Mashi? Why don't you go and mind your own business?'

Aunt thought she understood the hidden meaning in her niece's hint. So she now spoke more venomously than before.

'Don't be silly, Rama', she said. 'Unlike you people, I don't have any unnecessary scruple in doing what has to be done after all. Why did Beni run away like that? He should've told this man, "Look here, we're neither your employees nor your tenants that we should go to your house to do all sorts of chores. The whole village has heaved a sigh of relief at Tarini's death." It'd have been

6

manly on Beni's part to have told him all this to his face instead of leaving it to us women to do it.' Ramesh continued to stand still, like one dazed. Indeed, all this unpleasantness was beyond his worst dreams. There was a sudden clanking of the iron chain inside the kitchen, but nobody paid any heed to it.

Looking at the mute and extremely pale face of Ramesh, Rama's aunt yet said, 'Well, I wouldn't like to insult a Brahmin's son through servants. Go, but be more cautious in your dealings in future. You're no longer a child that you may enter into someone's house and crave indulgence. I tell you finally my Rama'll never go to your house, not even to wash her feet there!'

Ramesh now woke up, as if from sleep, and such a long, deep sigh came out of his broad chest that he himself was startled. Standing behind the kitchen door, Rama lifted her face and looked up at him.

After a moment's hesitation, Ramesh turned towards the kitchen and said, 'As it's not at all possible for you to go, it can't be helped. But believe me, Rani, I didn't know all this. If I've given you offence, I've done so unknowingly. Please forgive me.' Slowly Ramesh moved away.

There was no response from the person inside the room and Ramesh had no inkling of the fact that the person, from whom he had begged forgiveness, had continued to gaze at his face silently all this time.

Beni came back immediately. He had not gone away, but was just hiding outside. As soon as his eyes met the aunt's, his face lit up and burst forth in a broad smile. He came nearer and said, 'Indeed, Aunt, you've given him a fine talking-to! Honestly, I couldn't have done it. I say, Rama, this job could never have been done by a servant or watchman. I saw from my hiding that the fellow went away with a face as dark as the thunder-clouds of monsoon. Aunt has undoubtedly been most effective!'

'Well, we know all that', retorted aunt sharply, in an

aggrieved tone. 'But it'd have been much better if you'd told him all this yourself, instead of slipping away and throwing the burden on us two women. And, if you couldn't say all this, why didn't you stand by my side and hear what I told him? I must say that it wasn't right of you to have sneaked off like that!'

Beni's smile faded at the aunt's sharp tone. He could not think of any satisfactory answer to this accusation. But he did not have to think long. Suddenly Rama, who had been silent all this while, spoke to her aunt from inside the room, 'After all, Aunt, it's best that you've spoken yourself. Nobody else could've spoken so venomously like you.'

Both the aunt as well as Beni were astounded. Aunt turned towards the kitchen and screamed, 'What did you say?'

'Nothing!' snapped Rama. 'You've had to interrupt your prayers so many times, why don't you go now and finish them? Won't the cooking be done today?'

Saying this, Rama came out of the kitchen and, without another word, crossed the porch and entered a room. Beni whispered drily, 'What's the matter, Aunt?'

'How should I know? How can a maid-servant like me understand the temper of a queen?' replied the aunt. She then went and sat down to her prayers, her face dark with anger and grief – and perhaps began to recite the name of God in silence.

Beni quietly left the place.

CHAPTER
2

There is a short history behind the acquisition of this Kuanpur estate, which may be relevant here.

About a hundred years ago, the high-class Brahmin Balaram Mukharji came to this part of Bengal from Vikrampur, along with his namesake Balaram Ghoshal, and settled here. Besides being a high-class Brahmin, Mukharji was also a clever man. He acquired this property through his marriage and service under the Burdwan Raj, and also by other means. Ghoshal also married in this part of the country, but he was able to achieve nothing except beget children, and so passed his days in poverty and misery. It was on the occasion of Ghoshal's marriage that a misunderstanding developed between the two friends. Ultimately the estrangement reached such a height that although they lived in the same village, the two friends did not see each other during long twenty years. Even on the day of Balaram Mukharji's death, Ghoshal did not call on the bereaved family.

But on the next day a strange story was heard. It transpired that, before his death, Balaram Mukharji had divided his entire property equally between his own son and the sons of his friend. Since then the two families – the Mukharjis and the Ghoshals – had been enjoying the Kuanpur estate. They prided themselves as landowners and the villagers also did not question their claim.

When our story begins, the Ghoshal family had already broken up. Tarini, the younger of the two Ghos-

9

hal brothers, had suddenly died about a week before. He had gone to the district headquarters in connection with some lawsuits pending in the court. All on a sudden he received sommons from some unknown higher court and, in obedience to it, silently departed – without caring for the result of his pending cases. This caused a stir both inside and outside the village. Beni Ghoshal, the son and heir of Tarini's elder brother, secretly heaved a sigh of relief at his uncle's death, and more secretly began to form a clique so as to spoil his uncle's funeral ceremony. The uncle and the nephew had not cared to see each other's face even once during the last ten years.

Tarini had lost his wife long ago. Having sent his son Ramesh to his maternal uncle's house, Tarini managed his household with the help of servants, and kept himself busy with litigations. Ramesh received the sad news of his father's death at the Roorkee Engineering College and arrived at the empty house, after a long time, the previous afternoon, to perform the last rites of his father.

The house of ceremonies was busy with preparations for the obsequies due in only two more days – on the next Thursday. Some of the elders from other villages had started arriving, by ones and twos, but so far not a single person from his own village of Kuanpur had paid him a visit. Ramesh knew the reason why and feared that perhaps in the end nobody would turn up. Only Bhairab Acharjya and members of his family were already there, helping him. Although Ramesh had little hope that the Brahmins of his village would attend the ceremony, he had made arrangements befitting a rich man.

Today he remained busy inside the house for quite a long time. Coming out on some business, he found that some old gentlemen had already arrived and were enjoying a smoke, seated on the mattress in the drawing room. He came over and was about to say something polite to them when he heard a noise. He turned round and found that a very old man, accompanied by five or six children, was entering the house, coughing all the time. He had a dirty piece of cloth draped round his shoulders and a pair of huge spectacles perched on his nose, bound at the back of his head with a string. His hair and moustache were all white, but turned coppery by tobacco smoke. He came forward, peered at Ramesh from behind his oversize glasses for a moment, and without uttering a single word, burst into tears. Ramesh could not recognize him, but felt distressed all the same, and coming closer, clasped his hands. At once the man spoke out in a husky voice.

'Ramesh, my son,' he began. 'I never even dreamt that Tarini would give us the slip so soon. However, as one belonging to the Chatterjee family, I'm not the man who'd tell a lie out of fear for anybody. On my way I met your cousin Beni Ghoshal and told him on his face, "Our Ramesh has made elaborate arrangements for the funeral ceremony. Let alone do so, nobody has even seen such arrangement before in this part of the country."' He added after a pause, 'Many a rascal may come to you and slander me, but remember that this Dharmadas is a servant of Virtue and none else.' So saying, the old man proceeded towards the sitting room and abandoning all the proclaimed merit snatched the *hookah* from the hands of Govinda Ganguly, took a long pull at it, and burst forth into a fit of violent cough.

Dharmadas had not exaggerated. It was true that nobody else had arranged things on such a grand scale in this locality before. Confectioners had been brought from Calcutta. They were busy making sweets in one corner of the courtyard. Some of the neighbourhood children had crowded around them. Faithful Bhairab Acharjya was seated on the porch adjacent to the House

11

of Worship cutting out cloth and arranging them in bundles for distribution among the poor. Some people were squatting in front of that porch. They were calculating the unnecessary expenditure on this account and were silently deriding Ramesh for being such a fool. Having heard about the ceremony, some poor people were flocking to the house – some of them had even covered long distances. Tarini's employees and tenants had also come. The house was full. Some were quarrelling among themselves and some were making noise for nothing. The wastefulness on all sides seemed to further aggravate Dharmadas's cough.

Embarrassed at what Dharmadas had said, Ramesh was about to say something when Dharmadas stopped him by waving his hands and rattled on for some time. However, the words were all muffled by constant cough and Ramesh could not understand a single word of what Dharmadas said.

Govinda Ganguly, who was the first man to have come, could have said all these flattering things to Ramesh, which Dharmadas was now saying. He felt unhappy at the thought of having missed that opportunity. However, he was not the man to miss it again. He now started hastily, 'You see, Dharmadas-da, yesterday I set out with the intention of coming here, but I couldn't. Beni saw me coming this way and started shouting, "Govinda Uncle, please step in and have a smoke." First I thought there was no need to go. Then it suddenly occurred to me that I might as well find out what Beni was up to. Do you know, Ramesh, what he told me? He said, "Uncle, I see you've all become Ramesh's patrons, but are you sure people'll attend the ceremony?" Why should I spare him? He may be a rich man, but our Ramesh is no less. Nobody can expect to have even a handful of flattened rice from his house. I said in reply, "Beni Babu, this is the path. You may as well stand and watch the way the beggars are being fed.

Ramesh may be young, but he has a large heart! I've grown old, but in all my life I've never seen such grand arrangements before." But I must say, Dharmadas-da, that by ourselves we wouldn't have been able to do anything. It's Tarini-da who's getting his own work done from heaven. He was none other than an angel expelled from heaven by some curse.'

Dharmadas tried his best to stop his cough, but failed and went on coughing. Seeing that Ganguly was telling all the choicest words to this young, inexperienced landowner, and that too, in his presence, Dharmadas was desperately trying to stop his cough and say something better.

Ganguly went on, 'You're indeed a very near relation of mine, my son. Your mother was my own cousin— my father's sister's husband's younger brother's daughter. The Banerjis of Radhanagar...well, all that was known to Tarini-da. Whenever he needed me, I was sent – for any function or lawsuit or for giving evidence in a court.'

With the utmost effort Dharmadas was at last able to stop his cough. He now cried with a grimace, 'Why talk rubbish, Govinda? Cough – cough – cough – I'm not a child. I know everything. Some years back, when you were asked to give evidence, you said you didn't have shoes and it wasn't possible for you to go barefoot – cough – cough – Tarini immediately bought a pair of shoes for two-and-a-half rupees. You used the shoes all right, but gave false evidence in favour of Beni – cough – cough – cough.'

Govinda glared angrily with blood-shot eyes, 'Did I ?'

'Didn't you?'

'You're a damn liar!'

'Your father's a liar!'

Govinda sprang up waving his broken umbrella menacingly, 'You, bastard!'

Dharmadas also jumped up raising his stick, gave a roar, and fell into a fit of violent cough. Ramesh hur-

13

riedly intervened. He stood between them, completely astounded. Dharmadas lowered his stick and sat down, still coughing.

'I'm almost an elder brother to him, and this is how the bastard behaves with me!' cried Dharmadas.

'Oh, what a grand elder brother of mine!' shouted Govinda Ganguly. He then rolled up his umbrella and sat down.

The confectioners from Calcutta left their work and stared at them. Attracted by the shouts, those who were engaged in some work near by came running to enjoy the fun. Even the children left their play and gaped at them. And Ramesh standing right in the middle became dumb with shame and amazement. Not a single word escaped his lips. What was this? Both were aged persons – Brahmins too! How could they start abusing each other like low, vulgar people, and on such petty matters! Seated on the porch behind the pile of cloth, Bhairab had seen all, heard everything. He now got up and addressed Ramesh:

'About four hundred pieces of cloth are ready. Do you think we'll need more?'

Ramesh was too bewildered to give any reply. Bhairab noticed this and smiled. He then said in a tone of mild reproach, 'For shame, Mr. Ganguly! You've completely shocked the Master. Please, sir, don't take it so seriously. Such things do happen. Big ceremonies often witness fights and also bloodshed. But after some time everything settles down. Come on, get up, Mr. Chatterjee , come and see whether any more cloth is needed.'

Before Dharmadas could give any reply, Govinda Ganguly sat erect and said with an enthusiastic nod, 'Oh yes, yes, such things do happen! And in plenty! Otherwise why should such ceremonies be called grand affairs? Don't you know, according to the sacred scriptures, a marriage can't be held without the exchange of a million words! That year – you'll certainly remember,

14

Bhairab – how Raghab Bhattarcharjya and Haran Chatterjee fought and broke each other's heads over their respective share of the votive tray, during the consecration ceremony of a tree for Jadu Mukharji's daughter, Rama.... Now Bhairab, I think that young master's decision in this matter hasn't been a wise one. Distributing clothes to those low-caste fellows is as good as pouring ghee on burnt out fire. A pair of *dhotis* to each adult Brahmin and a piece to each Brahmin child would have brought him much more fame. I would suggest, Son, that'd be more reasonable. What d'you say, Dharmadas-da?'

Nodding his head in complete agreement, Dharmadas said to Ramesh, 'I think that's a very good suggestion ! No matter how much you give to these fellows, they'll never praise you. That's why they are called "low-born", isn't it? Don't you understand that?'

Ramesh had been silent all this time. But now the discussion over the distribution of cloth utterly shocked him. It was not the soundness or otherwise of the suggestion, but what cut him to the quick was that these two old Brahmins were not in the least ashamed or sorry for their most deplorable conduct in the presence of the very same people whom they called 'low-born'. Noticing that Bhairab was still looking at him, Ramesh said briefly, 'Let's have two hundred pieces more'.

'Oh, yes! How can you possibly manage with less? Now Bhairab, I think I must come and help you. How long will you work single-handed?' Without waiting for anybody's consent, Govinda went over to the porch and sat down near the heap of cloth.

As Ramesh turned towards the house, Dharmadas took him aside and whispered a lot of things into his ears. Ramesh simply nodded in assent and went in. While arranging the pieces of cloth, Govinda Ganguly noticed all this through the corners of his eyes.

'Where's the dear boy?' called out a thin, old, clean-shaven Brahmin, as he entered the courtyard. He was accompanied by three children. The eldest was a daughter. She was clad in a striped, completely wornout sari. The two boys were completely naked, except for a waist band. Everyone looked up. Govinda Ganguly welcomed him. 'Ah Dinu-da, do come in and sit. How lucky we are that you've come at last! The boy will wear himself out, unless you...'

Dharmadas looked at Govinda with a frown, but the latter paid no heed to it and continued, 'But you don't even step in this direction, Dada.' He then passed on the *hookah*. Dinu Bhattacharji sat down and after one or two pulls at the already burnt-out tobacco said, 'But I was away. I had gone to my father-in-law's house to fetch my wife. But where's the dear boy? I'm told he's making grand arrangements. At the marketplace of the neighbouring village I gathered that after the funeral dinner is over, every Brahmin will be given sixteen pieces of *luchi* and four pairs of *sandesh* to take home.'

Govinda lowered his voice and said, 'And perhaps a piece of cloth also. Oh, here's dear Ramesh! I was just telling Dinu-da that through the blessings of your forefathers, arrangements have been made as best possible. But Beni seems determined to spoil the whole show. He has already sent a man to me twice. Of course, you may leave aside my case; I'm intimately related to you and blood is thicker than water. But what about persons like Dinu-da and Dharmadas-da? They too can't afford to forsake you, can they? Dinu-da had heard about the ceremony on his way back and immediately hurried to this place. Hey, you, Shasthicharan, let's have more tobacoo! Now, Ramesh, my son, will you please step this way -- I'll have a word with you.' Taking Ramesh to one side, Govinda whispered, 'I think Dharmadas's wife is inside, isn't she? For Heaven's sake, take care, take care! However much that roguish Brahmin flatters, you must never hand over the keys to his wife, never! She'll

16

remove half the quantity of *ghee*, rice, flour, oil, salt in no time. But you needn't worry at all! I'll go and send your maternal aunt immediately. Once she takes charge of the store-room, you won't lose anything –not even a wisp of hay.'

Ramesh nodded and said, 'All right', and fell silent. His surprise knew no bounds. How on earth could this fellow Govinda guess what Dharmadas had told him so secretly – that his wife would be coming to take charge of the store-room! Strange!

The two naked sons of Dinu came running and leaned over his shoulders. 'Father, we want sweets', they cried.

Dinu looked once at Ramesh and again at Govinda. 'Where'll I get sweets, my boys?' he said.

'Why? They're making it there', they said, pointing to the confectioners.

Dharmadas's grandchildren also came running and surrounding the withered old man started in a whine, 'We also want sweets, grandpa.'

'All right! All right!' said Ramesh, hastily coming forward. 'You see Mr. Acharjya, these children have come without eating anything in the afternoon... Hey, you, what's your name? Let's have that tray over here!'

As soon as the confectioner came with the tray, all the children fell upon it. They were in such a terrible hurry that they would not even allow him to distribute the sweets. At the sight of the children eating *sandesh* with great relish, Dinu's dry eyes became moist and keen. 'O Khendi,' he said. 'Good, you're eating *sandesh*, but tell us how it tastes!'

'Excellent, Father!' replied Khendi and went on chewing.

Dinu grinned and shook his head. 'Ha! As if you've any sense of taste!' he said. 'Anything sweet is good enough for you! Hey, confectioner, how did the latest ones turn out? I think, Govinda, there's still a bit of sunlight... what d'you say?'

17

Without caring to look up the confectioner promptly said, 'Yes sir! Sure there is! There's still a long time before sunset. The evening prayers are still...'

'Well, then let Govinda taste one *sandesh* and say how good you Calcutta confectioners are! No, no, why are you giving me also? Then give only a half! That'll do...Hey, Shasthicharan, get a glass of water...Let me wash my hands.'

Ramesh called out, 'Bring some plates also from the house, Shasthicharan.'

As ordered by his master, the servant brought three plates and glasses from the house and in no time these three aged malaria-stricken Brahmins finished half the quantity of *sandesh* from the huge tray.

Dinanath took a long breath and said, 'Yes, they're good indeed, these Calcutta confectioners! What d'you say, Dharmadas-da?'

Dharmadas had not yet finished. Although his voice was not audible through the mass of *sandesh* still in his mouth, it became quite clear that he too was of the same opinion.

'Yes, undoubtedly expert confectioners', remarked Govinda, being the last to finish. He was about to wash his hands when the confectioner requested humbly, 'When you've taken so much trouble, Sir, won't you please try the *mihidana* also?'

'*Mihidana*? Where's it? Let's have some.'

Mihidana was served and Ramesh silently wondered at the quantity of this new sweet-meat devoured after so many pieces of *sandesh*.

Dinanath stretched his hand out to his daughter and called, 'O Khendi, come on, have some *mihidana*.'

'I can't eat any more, Father.'

'Oh yes, I'm sure you can. Why not take a sip of water and moisten your throat? The sweet taste must have marred your appetite. And if you really can't eat any more, tie it in the corner of your sari; you can eat it tomorrow morning.... We really had our fill, my son.

18

The taste was like nectar! But are you serving just two kinds of sweets, my Son?'

There was no need for Ramesh to speak. The confectioner said, enthusiastically, 'No sir! There's *rasogolla*, *khirmohans* also.'

'What ! *Khirmohan*! How's it you haven't shown it to us yet?'

Dinanath looked up at Ramesh's surprised face and continued, 'Ah! How I had enjoyed the *Khirmohan* at the Bose house at Radhanagar! The taste of it still lingers on my tongue. You may not believe it, Son, but I'm extremely fond of *Khirmohan*'.

Ramesh smiled an amused smile and nodded. It was not really difficult for him to believe this. His servant Rakhal was going out on some errand at that time. Ramesh called out to him and said, 'Mr. Acharjya is probably inside. Just go and ask him to bring some *Khirmohan* along.'

The evening was perhaps already over. Yet the three Brahmins sat expectantly for the *Khirmohan*. Rakhal came back and said, 'Sir, the store-room is already locked; it won't be opened again today.'

Ramesh felt a bit annoyed. He said, 'Go and say that I've asked for it.'

Govinda Ganguly had noticed Ramesh's annoyance. He now said with a frown, 'Dinu-da, have you marked Bhairab's impertinence? It's as they say, the aunt is more solicitous than the mother! That's why I say...'

Rakhal interrupted him and said, 'What can Mr.Acharjya do? The Mistress has come over from the other house and shut the store-room.'

Both Dharmadas and Govinda were startled.

'Who's come? Beni Babu's mother?'

Ramesh asked, in surprise, 'What ! Has aunty come?'

'Yes, sir. As soon as she came, she put the two store-rooms – both the large and the samll – under lock and key.'

Agreeably surprised and delighted, Ramesh left in a hurry, without another word, and went inside.

CHAPTER
3

'Aunty!' Bishweshwari heard him and came out of the store-room.

Considering Beni's age, his mother's ought to have been over fifty, but she did not look a day more than forty. Ramesh looked at her with a fixed stare. Her skin still had the colour of pure gold. At one time Bishweshwari was noted in this part of the country for her extraordinary beauty. That resplendent beauty was still visible in all its glory in her well preserved and graceful body. Her hair was close-cropped, but a few curling locks hung over her forehead. Her lips, chin, cheeks, and forehead were all exquisite – as if they had been specially chiselled by some master sculptor. The most attractive thing about her were her two wonderful eyes. They seemed to cast a spell on anyone who looked at them.

At one time Bishweshwari used to love Ramesh and, particularly, his dead mother very dearly. It was before their own sons were born. When the two young sisters-in-law, ill-treated by their mother-in-law and her daughter, used to sit side by side in a corner of the house shedding tears, a bond of love was formed. Later came family quarrels, partition of the family property, litigations, and all sorts of storm and stress that swept over their two houses. The heat of the quarrel loosened the old tie, but could not completely sever it. When Bishweshwari had entered the store-room of her younger sister-in-law today, after so many years, and

20

looked at the old pots and pans, which had once been so carefully arranged by her, tears welled up in her eyes. When Ramesh called her, she quickly wiped the tears before she came out. Looking at her two reddish and moist eyes, Ramesh was bewildered for a moment. Aunty noticed this. Possibly that was why, even though her heart cried out in anguish at the sight of the mournful youth standing before her, who had lost his father only a few days ago, she did not give the least expression to her sorrow. Rather she forced a smile on her lips and said, 'Can you recognise me, Ramesh?'

Ramesh could not give any reply; his lips quivered. He remembered how after his mother's death, until he was sent to his maternal uncle's house, Aunty had looked after him with loving care and had been most reluctant to let him go. He also remembered that when he had gone to meet her the other day, she did not see him and he was told that she was not at home. Later, in Rama's house, her aunt's extreme severe reproaches, both in Beni's presence and in his absence, convinced him that there was not a single soul in this village whom he might call his own.

Bishweshwari looked at Ramesh for a moment. 'No, my dear, this won't do', she admonished. 'You mustn't lose heart at a time like this.' There was no trace of tenderness in her voice. Ramesh immediately controlled himself. He felt that nothing could be more distressing than to expect sympathy where there was none. He said, 'No, I haven't, Aunty! I would've carried on somehow; why did you trouble yourself to come?'

Aunty said with a smile, 'Well, you didn't ask me to come, did you? So I don't have to justify my coming. Now listen to me. I won't allow any more food to be taken out of the store-room before the ceremony. While going, I'll hand over the keys to you and take them back from you when I come again tomorrow morning. Mind you, don't give the keys to anyone else! By the way, did you meet your Dada that day?'

Ramesh was perplexed. He was not quite sure whether she was aware of her son's attitude towards him. He replied, after a pause, 'Dada wasn't at home at that time.'

A shadow of anxiety had fallen across Aunty's face immediately after putting the question. Ramesh noticed clearly that with his answer the shadow was lifted, and cheerfulness filled her countenance again. She now said smilingly, with a tinge of gentle reproof, 'Oh, my goodness! Simply because he wasn't at home that day, you didn't think it necessary to go again! I know that he isn't pleased with you, but you mustn't fail in your duty. Go, Ramesh, go and request him to come. After all, he's your elder brother. You needn't feel ashamed to bow down before him. Moreover, this is such a time of distress for you, dear, that you should make up with others at any cost. Listen, my boy, go again. He's probably at home now.'

Ramesh remained silent. The reason for this insistence was not quite clear to him. Neither could he shake off his misgivings from his mind. Bishweshwari came closer and said in a low voice, 'Those who are seated outside, I know them much better than you do. Don't listen to what they say. Come, let's go to your Dada, just for once!'

Ramesh shook his head and said, 'No, Aunty, that cannot be. Besides, those seated outside, whoever they might be, are the ones who are nearest to me now.'

He would have gone on, but a glance at Aunty's face suddenly held him back. It seemed to him that Aunty's face had turned gloomier than even the darkness of the evening around them.

After some time she heaved a sigh and said, 'Well, then let me go. If it isn't at all possible for you to go and meet him, what's the good of talking about it? However, you needn't worry, dear, your work won't suffer. I'll be

22

around again early tomorrow morning.' Calling her maid, Bishweshwari slowly went out through the back door. It was clear to her that Ramesh had met Beni in the mean time and there had been some unpleasantness between them.

After her departure, Ramesh stood silently for some time, gazing at the path she had taken. When at last he came out of the room, with a heavy heart, Govinda enquired eagerly, 'The Mistress had come, hadn't she?'

Ramesh nodded.

'Heard she's locked up the store-room and taken the keys along?'

Ramesh again nodded in assent. Because, when she left, Bishweshwari had indeed taken the keys along with her. Govinda immediately said, 'Did you see, Dharmadas-da! Just what I had told you! Well, did you make out her intentions, Son?'

Ramesh felt a terrible anger rising within himself, but realizing his helpless condition, he controlled himself and kept quiet.

Poor Dinu Bhattacharji had not yet left. He was not clever enough like the others. He did not think it proper to go without conveying his thanks to the man who had just given him and his children a sumptuous feast of sweets, without showering his blessing upon him and without singing praise of his forefathers in the general presence. The poor Brahmin now said, innocently, 'Where's the difficulty in understanding her intention, brother? She put the store-room under lock and key and took away the keys so that nobody else should get into the store. After all, she knows everything.'

Govinda had already become annoyed. These remarks from foolish Dinu made him furious. He rapped out, 'You don't understand anything! Why must you always speak! What do you know of these matters that you come forward to explain things?'

This scolding aggravated Dinu's foolishness. He replied, hotly, 'What's there to understand in this simple matter? Didn't you hear that the Mistress has locked up the store herself? Who's there to say anything about that?'

Govinda flared up and shouted, 'Why don't you go home, Bhattacharji! You've already had more than your share of the things for which you came hurrying. You and your brood ate, and are also carrying sweets home. Then why stay any longer? *Khirmohan* you can have only day after tomorrow... there'll be nothing more today. Now get going and leave us alone! We've a lot to do!'

Dinu was ashamed and embarrassed. Ramesh became mortified and angry. Govinda was about to say something more when Ramesh's calm but firm tone checked him. 'What's the matter with you, Mr. Ganguly? Why are you going about insulting people for nothing.'

Govinda was at first taken aback. But the next moment he simpered drily. 'Who did I insult, Son? Well, why don't you ask him whether I've spoken the truth or not. He must know that I'm more than a match for him. Did you notice, Dharmadas-da, the impertinence of this fellow Dinu? Well, we'll see...'

What Dharmadas had noticed he kept to himself, but Ramesh was astounded by the shamelessness and audacity of the man. Then Dinu, turning towards Ramesh, said, 'No, my Son, Govinda has spoken the truth. Everyone knows how poor I am. Unlike them, I don't even possess a strip of land. In a way, I maintain my family through begging and borrowing. God hasn't given me the means to buy food to provide for my children... only when there's some ceremony in a rich man's house, they get a chance to eat. When Tarini-da was alive, he was fond of feeding us all. I can tell you for sure that he's pleased to see from heaven that you've fed us sumptuously.'

Suddenly tears welled up in Dinu's dry and sunken

eyes and rolled down his cheeks, in the presence of all. Ramesh turned his face and looked aside. Dinu wiped his tears away with the dirty and tattered ends of his scarf and continued, 'Not only I, but so many other poor people who came to seek help from Tarini-da never went back disappointed. But who knows that? – none! Because his left hand didn't know what his right hand did! But I'll bother you no more. Come Khendi, my child. Come, Haridhan, let's go home now. We'll come in the morning again. What more can I say, Ramesh, my Son. Live long, and may you be like your father!'

Ramesh went along a few steps, and then, in a voice brimming with emotion, said, 'Mr. Bhattacharji, please be kind to me for the next two or three days. I hesitate to say this – but I'd consider myself fortunate if Haridhan's mother could come over to my place once.'

Hastily taking Ramesh's hands in his own, Mr. Bhattacharji said, almost in tears, 'I'm a very poor man, Ramesh. I feel awfully embarrassed when you speak to me in this way.' The old man then moved away slowly, accompanied by his children.

Ramesh came back. Aware of his momentary rudeness to Govinda, he was trying to say something when Govinda stopped him and spoke excitedly, 'I do consider this ceremony to be mine, Ramesh. Even if you didn't ask me to come, I'd have had to come of my own accord and do everything. You can see for yourself, Son, that we two brothers, Dharmadas-da and I, haven't waited for your formal invitation.'

Dharmadas was coughing after a smoke. Leaning on his stick he raised himself. His face was flushed with a spasm. Waving both hands, he said, 'Listen to me, Ramesh; we aren't like Beni Ghoshal! We aren't bastards!'

Ramesh was shocked at the man's vile abuse, but did not lose his temper. He had learnt, within this short time, that want of education and long-standing habit had made these people use vulgar language without the least hesitation and they had no idea how reprehensible their conduct appeared to others.

Remembering Aunty's earnest request, and the sorrowful expression on her face at the time of her departure, Ramesh decided to go and meet Beni. It was almost eight at night when he arrived outside Beni's House of Worship. It seemed as if a fight was going on inside. Govinda Ganguly was making the loudest noise. Though standing outside, Ramesh could hear all that Govinda was saying. 'I can bet, Beni Babu, if he doesn't turn pauper in two days' time, you may very well change my name! You've just heard of his acting like a nawab, haven't you? We all know that Tarini Ghoshal died without a copper; then why this pomp? If you've enough cash in hand, spend it as you like; but whoever heard of anyone mortgaging his property for performing the obsequies of his father? I never heard of such a thing before! I tell you, Benimadhab Babu, this fellow must've borrowed at least three thousand rupees from the firm of the Nandy's!'

'Then we must get the confirmation, Govinda Uncle!' said Beni enthusiastically.

Govinda lowered his voice a little. 'Just wait a little, Son. Let me establish myself – and then... who's there standing outside? Why, it's dear Ramesh! But why did you take the trouble of coming yourself, so late at night when we're all here to do your bidding?'

Without paying any heed to him, Ramesh advanced towards Beni and said, 'Dada, I've come to you'.

Beni was completely nonplussed and could not reply. Govinda immediately broke in, 'Of course, why shouldn't you? You can come a hundred times. After all this is almost your own house. And an elder brother is almost like a father. That's why we've come to tell Beni Babu, "Well, Beni Babu, let the old misunderstanding end with Tarini-da's death! Why prolong it? You two brothers should now be reconciled and live in amity. This'll give us the greatest satisfaction." What d'you say, Haldar Uncle? But what's this, you're still standing? Hey! Who's there! Get a woollen rug for him to sit upon! No, Beni Babu, this won't do! You're the elder brother! You're all in all! It won't do for you to remain aloof. Besides, when your mother has herself visited...'

Beni was startled. 'Did mother go there?'

Noticing Beni's surprised look, Govinda was filled with glee. But he did not express his feelings openly. Assuming the air of an innocent, good-natured man, he began to enlarge upon the subject. 'It wasn't just a courtesy call either. She took charge of the store and did everything. Well, that's only natural! Who else is there to do it?'

Everybody kept mum. Govinda heaved a sigh and continued, 'Indeed, there's none like your mother in the whole village... nor is there likely to be one! Well, Beni Babu, it may sound like flattery saying all this before you, but I must say that if there's anyone like goddess Lakshmi in our village, it's your mother! Few people have a mother like her!' He sighed again and suddenly turning grave, fell silent.

After a long silence, Beni mumbled, almost to himself, 'All right...'

Govinda pressed again. 'No, no, Beni Babu, a mere "all right" won't do. You've to go there; look to all arrangements personally; the entire responsibility rests on you. By the way, now that all of us are present here, why not prepare the list of invitees? What d'you say, dear Ramesh? Isn't that right, Mr. Haldar? Dharmadas-da, why are you silent? Well, you know who's to be invited and who's to be excluded.'

Ramesh stood up and said, humbly and respectfully, 'Dada, if you could just come once...'

Beni replied gravely, 'As mother has already gone, it's

as good as my going.... What d'you say, Govinda Uncle?'

Before Govinda could say anything, Ramesh intervened. 'I wouldn't like to press you, Dada, but if it isn't inconvenient for you, please come once and see if everything is in order.'

Beni was quiet. As Govinda started to say something, Ramesh walked away. Govinda craned his neck and glanced outside. Then, almost in a whisper, he said, 'Did you notice the way he spoke, Beni Babu?' Beni was absent-minded, absorbed in his own thoughts. He did not reply.

As he walked down the path on his way home, Ramesh recollected all that Govinda had just said, and revulsion filled his mind. Half-way down, he stopped, turned back and entered Beni Ghoshal's house for the second time that night. The clamour inside the House of Worship had by now become more noisy and excited, but Ramesh had no inclination to listen to their talk. He went straight inside and called out, 'Aunty!'

Aunty was sitting silently in the darkness of the porch adjoining her room. She was surprised to hear Ramesh's voice so late at night.

'Ramesh? What's the matter?'

Ramesh climbed the steps to the porch. Aunty said quickly, 'Wait a bit, dear. Let them get a lamp.'

'There's no need for a lamp, Aunty. Please don't get up.' Saying this he sat down in one corner of the dark porch.

Aunty asked, 'Why did you have to come at this hour?'

Ramesh replied in a low voice, 'The invitations haven't yet been sent. I came to consult you about that.'

'There, you've got me into a nice fix! What do they say? Govinda Ganguly, Mr. Chatterjee ...?'

Ramesh interrupted her and said, 'I don't know what they say about it, Aunty —nor do I want to know. I'll do just as you say.'

Bishweshwari was surprised at this sudden warmth

28

in Ramesh's tone. She remained silent for some time, and then said, 'But you told me, these people were the nearest to you, didn't you? In any case, what does a woman's advice count for? Morever, in this village -- why only here, in other villages too – someone may not eat in the company of someone else, while another may not be on speaking terms with some others. Whenever a social occasion comes up, there's no end to worry. In a village, the most difficult job is to decide who's to be invited and who's to be left out!'

Ramesh did not feel greatly surprised. He had grown much wiser in these few days. Yet he asked, 'Why is it like this, Aunty?'

'That's a long story. If you remain here, you'll know all that yourself. Some are really guilty, while others are falsely accused. Besides, there are factions arising out of litigations, false evidence, etc. Had I gone to your house a couple of days earlier, I wouldn't have allowed you to make such elaborate arrangements. I keep worrying what's going to happen that day!' She heaved a deep sigh.

Ramesh could not fathom the depths of that sigh. Nor was it clear to him what the nature of the offence committed by some was and the false accusations against others. He said, excitedly, 'But I'm not in any way concerned with such disputes! I'm more or less a stranger here.... I've no enmity with anyone. So I feel, Aunty, that I should invite all the Brahmins and Sudras without any discrimination, without taking note of the factional disputes. But I can't do this without your approval. Please give me your permission, Aunty.'

Aunty remained silent for some time, absorbed in her thoughts, and then said, 'I can't give you such permission, Ramesh. That'll lead to serious trouble. I can't of course deny the truth in what you say. But it's not a simple question of what's right and what's wrong. One whom the society shuns, mustn't be invited that way.

Whatever may be the defects of the society, one must obey its injunctions. Otherwise it'll lose all its powers, either for good or for evil.... and that won't do at all, Ramesh.'

Perhaps if he had thought over the matter coolly, Ramesh could not have denied this altogether. But the intrigues and meanness of the leaders of this same society were still burning in his heart like a flame of fire. He replied contemptuously, 'Who constitute the society in this village? Men like Dharmadas and Govinda – isn't it? Wouldn't it be far better if such a society possessed no powers at all, Aunty?'

Aunty noticed Ramesh's excitement, but she replied coolly, 'They aren't the only persons, Ramesh. Your Dada, Beni, is also one of the elders of this society.'

Ramesh remained silent. She repeated, 'So I suggest you act according to their advice, Ramesh. You've just returned home; it wouldn't he wise to antagonize them so soon."

In his great excitement, Ramesh did not consider after how much deliberate consideration Bishweshwari had offered him the advice. He said, 'You yourself told me just a while ago that so many factors are responsible for the factions and disputes here. Perhaps personal grudge is the main reason. Besides, as I know nothing about the real or imaginary fault of anyone, I believe it'd be wrong on my part to insult someone by excluding him from the list of invitees.'

Aunty said, with a faint smile, 'Oh, you mad boy! But I'm also your elder... almost like a mother to you. Don't you think you would be doing wrong by disobeying me?'

'I'm sorry, Aunty, but I've finally decided to invite everyone.'

Bishweshwari looked displeased; perhaps she was annoyed at heart. She retorted, 'Oh, then your request for my advice was just a pretence!'

Ramesh noticed Aunty's annoyance, but was not deflected from his resolve. After a brief pause he said, quietly, 'I know, Aunty, that if I followed the right path, you'd gladly give me your blessings. I ...'

But before he could finish, Bishweshwari cried, 'But, at the same time you should've known that I couldn't turn against my own son!'

This gave Ramesh a rude shock. Whatever he might have said openly, in his heart of hearts he had been craving for a mother's affection from Aunty, since the previous day. Now he felt that only her own son was firmly established in his seat in Aunty's heart, and there was no place for him there. He remained silent for a long time. He then rose to his feet and said in a voice choked with emotion and injured affection, 'Till yesterday that was what I knew, Aunty! That's why I told you that I'd somehow carry on, you needn't come. I didn't even have the courage to ask you to come over.'

Aunty noticed Ramesh's aggrieved tone, but she did not say anything more, and continued to sit silently in the darkness. After some time when Ramesh got up to leave, she said, 'Well, then just wait a little. Let me bring the keys of your store-room.' She brought the keys from inside her room and threw the bunch down at Ramesh's feet. Ramesh stood for some time like one dazed. He then took a long breath and, picking up the keys, slowly went his way.

Only a few hours ago he had said to himself, 'I needn't be afraid any more. I've my Aunty with me.' But not even a night passed before he had to say to himself again, with a sigh, 'No, I've none to call my own. Even Aunty has forsaken me.'

31

CHAPTER
4

The funerary ceremony had just finished outside. Ramesh had got up from his seat and was trying to get to know his guests. Inside the house, leaves were being laid for the lunch. All on a sudden he heard an uproar from inside the house, and rushed in. Many of the assembled guests also came along with him.

Near the door of the kitchen, a young widow of twenty-five or twenty-six stood, cowering in fear. She stood facing the door, hiding her face from others, while an elderly woman had planted herself protectively in front of her. She was shouting angrily with red hot eyes and flushed face, and seemed to be spitting fire at Paran Haldar. As soon as the woman saw Ramesh, she shouted, 'Son, you're also one of the landowners of this village. I say, is this Khanti Bamni's daughter the only guilty woman in the whole village? Should we be punished as many times as they please simply because we've none to protect us?'

As soon as she saw Govinda she said, 'Didn't he collect a fine of ten rupees from me for the school fund on the occasion of the consecration ceremony of a tree in the Mukharji house? Didn't he realize the price of two pairs of goats from me when the village worshipped the goddess Shitala? Then? Why do they raise the old issue again and again and humiliate us?'

Ramesh was at a loss to understand what was going on. Govinda Ganguly got up from his seat and came forward to settle the dispute. Glancing once at Ramesh and then at the woman, he said, gravely: 'Well Khanto

Aunty, as you've mentioned my name, I must tell the truth. Govinda Ganguly is not the man to tell a lie, for anyone's sake, and the whole village knows it! It's a fact that your daughter underwent the prescribed expiatory rites, and we realized fine on behalf of the community. All that's correct. But we've not permitted her to take part in a social function like this. When she dies, we'll surely carry her body to the cremation ground, but...'

Khanto Aunty screamed, 'When your own daughter dies, go and cremate her —you needn't worry about my daughter! I say, Govinda, why d'you forget the affairs in your own family? What was the matter with that widow of your younger brother, who's making betel-rolls there in that room, may I ask? On what pilgrimage had she gone last year, that she came back one and a half months later, pale, anaemic and emaciated – as thin as a wick? But, that concerns a rich man's family, does it? Don't provoke me further, I can expose all of you! We too have reared children, we can find out what's what. You can't throw dust in our eyes!'

Govinda rushed at her like a madman. 'You despicable woman!' he cried, 'I'll teach you a lesson!'

But the despicable woman was not in the least frightened. Rather she advanced one or two steps and waving her arms and making faces said, 'You want to beat me up, eh? If you've the cheek to provoke this Khanti Bamni, she won't spare the reputation of any of you, I'm telling you! My daughter didn't enter the kitchen. Why did Mr. Haldar have to insult her all on a sudden like that even before she reached the door-steps? What about the scandal concerning his own son's mother-in-law? Wasn't she known to have come from a family of weavers? It's not that I was born yesterday! Should I tell more or will this be enough?'

Ramesh stood rooted to the spot, like a block of wood. Bhairab Acharjya hurried over and almost catching hold of Khanto's hands, spoke imploringly, 'That'll do, Aunty. Please stop now! Come Sukumari, my child, come with me and sit in the other room.'

33

Paran Haldar put his wrap back on his shoulders, stood up and shouted, 'I swear I'll not take a drop of water in this house until these whores are driven away! Govinda! Kalicharan! If you want to have anything to do with your uncle, leave this place at once and come with me. Beni Ghoshal was quite right when he warned me against coming here. Had I known that such harlots would be allowed to come here, I'd never have crossed the threshold of this house, risking the purity of my caste! Get up at once, Kali!'

In spite of the repeated requests from his uncle, Kalicharan remained glued to his seat, his head hanging low. He was a dealer in jute. About four years ago, an influential customer of his from Calcutta had eloped with his young widowed sister. The affair could not be kept a secret. It was suppressed for a short time on the pretext that the girl had gone to her father-in-law's and thence on a pilgrimage. Kali was afraid even to raise his head, lest that unfortunate episode should be raised by someone in the presence of so many.

But Govinda had not yet been pacified; he was still fuming and fretting. He again stood up and cried at the top of his voice, 'Whatever one may say, the fact remains that Beni Ghoshal, Paran Haldar and Jadu Mukharji's daughter are the leaders of the community in this place. We can't go against them. Young Ramesh has gone against the community by allowing these two tarts to enter his house. Unless he explains the reason why, we can't take even a drop of water in this house!'

One by one a number of persons placed their wraps on their shoulder and stood up. They all lived in the village. They knew very well which move would be the most advantageous in such a situation like this.

The Brahmins and other gentlemen who had been invited started making all sorts of remarks. Almost in tears, Bhairab and Dinu Bhattacharji tried their best to placate Govinda Ganguly, Paran Haldar, Khanto Aunty and her daughter, by turn, by earnest entreaties, by

34

almost falling at their feet. It seemed as if the entire ceremony was going to end in a fiasco. Exhausted by hunger and thirst and overwhelmed by this sudden unfortunate development, Ramesh was unable to utter a single word. He remained standing with a pale face, completely stunned.

'Ramesh!'

The startled gaze of all those assembled there turned upon Bishweshwari, who had come out of the storeroom, and now stood in its front. The border of her sari covered her head, but her face was uncovered. Ramesh saw that his Aunty had not really forsaken him – she had come of her own accord. The outsiders saw that this woman was none other than Bishweshwari, the 'Mistress of the Ghoshal family.

Purdah is not observed in villages as strictly as in towns. Yet, in spite of her advanced years, Bishweshwari was not ordinarily seen outside, either because she belonged to a wealthy family, or for some other reason of her own. So all of them were greatly surprised. Those who had only heard about her but had never seen her before, were astonished when they gazed at her striking eyes. Possibly she had come out into the open, suddenly, from a spurt of anger. But as soon as she perceived that so many eyes were turned on at her, she withdrew behind a pillar.

Aunty's clear and high-pitched voice shook Ramesh out of his bewilderment. He now came forward. She continued in the same clear and loud voice from behind the pillar, 'Ramesh, ask Mr. Ganguly not to threaten you; and tell Mr. Haldar in my name that all are my honoured guests; he had no business to insult Sukumari. I forbid anyone to indulge in shouting, abusing or making a racket in this house while the ceremony is going on! If it's inconvenient for anyone, he may go and sit elsewhere!'

Everybody heard this strict command from the Mistress of the Ghoshal family. It was not necessary for

Ramesh to say anything. He would not have been able to do so even if it were necessary. He did not even stop to see the impact of Aunty's action. Seeing that Aunty had taken the entire responsibility upon herself, he somehow checked his tears and hurriedly entered a room. Immediately tears started rolling down his cheeks in profuse streams. He had been extremely busy with the ritual throughout the day and had not had the time to find out who had come and who had not. But it was beyond his imagination that of all persons Aunty would come.

Those who had risen from their seats now sat down again. Only Govinda Ganguly and Paran Haldar remained standing, in an uneasy posture. Someone from the crowd spoke to them in a muffled voice, 'Better sit down, Uncle. Where else do you get sixteen pieces of *luchi* and four pairs of *sandesh* to take home? That too after a sumptuous feast?'

Paran Haldar slowly walked away. But, strangely enough, Govinda Ganguly actually sat down. But he pulled a long face all through and, when dinner was served, he did not eat his meal in the company of others on the pretext of supervising the arrangements. Those who noticed this were convinced that Govinda would not spare anyone so easily. But no further trouble arose. The quantity of food which each one of the Brahmins devoured that day had to be seen to be believed. Besides, each carried with him not a small quantity of food in the name of his absent children at home – Khudi, Patol, Nyara, Buro, etc.

It was past evening. All the business of the day was nearly over. Ramesh was standing absent-mindedly under a guava tree near the main gate. He was in a depressed mood. He saw Dinu Bhattacharji, bent down under the heavy weight of bundles of food which he was carrying home, slinking away with his children. Khendi was the first to notice Ramesh. Embarrassed like one

36

detected in the act of doing something wrong, she stopped, and said drily, 'Father, Babu is standing there...'

They were all a little flustered. From the way the girl had spoken, everything was clear to Ramesh. He would have run away had there been a way of escape. Since there was none, he came forward and said with a smile, 'Khendi, for whom are you carrying these things, dear?'

Apprehending that Khendi might not be able to give any satisfactory explanation for all the bundles they were carrying, Dinu came forward to give the reply, and said with a constrained smile, 'Oh, there're lots of poor children in our neighbourhood. I thought if I collected the leavings, I could distribute these among them... Well, it was abundantly clear to me today why all the people call that lady "the Mistress."'

Ramesh gave no reply to this, but came along up to the gate and then asked, suddenly, 'Well, Mr. Bhattacharji, you know everything in this locality. Could you tell me why there's so much ill-feeling in this village?'

Dinu clicked his tongue and shook his head several times. 'Alas, Son! Our Kuanpur isn't all that bad. What an awful state of affairs did I see at Khendi's uncle's place! There're not even twenty families in the village, Brahmins and others, but there're as many as four factions! Haranath Biswas sent his own nephew to jail because he had plucked two hog-plums from his tree! The condition is the same in every village. Besides, litigations have ruined them all... Khendi dear, will you take over the bundle and give Haridhan a rest?'

Ramesh again asked, 'Is there no remedy for this, Mr. Bhattacharji?'

How can there be any remedy, Son – isn't this the worst part of *Koli*, the Age of Unrighteousness. Bhattacharji heaved a sigh, and continued: 'But I can tell you one thing, Son. I travel around many places collecting charity...many are kind to me. I've seen that young men like you are generally charitably minded, it's only the old fogeys who have no kindness in their hearts. If one of them gets someone in his clutches, he doesn't spare him until he had plucked out his tongue.'

To show how this is done, Dinu lolled out his tongue in such a funny way that Ramesh began to laugh. But Dinu did not join Ramesh in his laughter. He said, 'This isn't a matter for laughter, Son... I am telling you the truth. I've grown old myself, but... oh, it's a long way you've come in darkness, Son!'

'That doesn't matter, Mr.Bhattacharji. Please continue.'

'What more shall I say, my dear? All villages are equally bad. That Govinda Ganguly... Just recounting the stories of his sins pollutes the mouth and one has to do penance. Khanto Bamni has only spoken the truth... yet people fear him. He has no match in committing fraud, giving false evidence and in hatching false cases. Beni Babu is his patron, so nobody has the guts to say anything against him. And he goes on merrily, misbehaving and defiling the purity of caste of others.'

Ramesh asked no more questions, but went on, walking silently with Dinu for quite some time.

'You may take it from me, Khanto Bamni is in for trouble. Govinda Ganguly! Paran Haldar! She has indeed stirred up a hornet's nest! But I must say that woman has guts. And why not? She goes from door to door selling puffed rice and knows the secrets of every house. If she is provoked again, there'll be no end of scandal. After all, every family has a skeleton in its cupboard. Even Beni Babu...'

Alarmed, Ramesh hastily stopped him. 'Please... Let's not talk about Dada.'

Dinu felt embarrassed, and said, 'Quite true, my dear. I'm a poor man; I really oughtn't to poke my nose in other people's affairs. If Beni Babu hears of this, my house will be set on fire...'

Ramesh again interrupted him, 'Mr. Bhattacharji, is your house still farther?'

'No, my Son, it isn't. My hut's just near the embankment. If some day you...'

'Oh, yes, I'll surely come.' Ramesh turned to go back. 'We'll meet again tomorrow morning. But, even afterwards, I'll be glad if you'll please come to my house now and then.' Ramesh turned and started walking away.

'May you live long! May you be like your father!' blessed Dinu Bhattacharji from the depths of his heart and then went his way, along with his children.

CHAPTER
5

Madhu Pal's shop was on the way to the river at one side of the marketplace. He was the only grocer in this part of the village. Ten or twelve days had already passed, yet the man had not turned up to receive payment of ten rupees due to him. Remembering this, Ramesh set out for the shop one morning. Madhu Pal received Ramesh with great respect and offered him a wicker stool on the verandah. When he learnt the reason for Ramesh's visit, Madhu's surprise knew no bounds. In all his life Madhu Pal had never known a single case in which a debtor came of his own accord to the creditor to clear his dues, nor had be even heard of such a thing before.

They had a long chat about all sorts of things. Madhu said, 'How can I run this shop, Babu? Dues like two annas, four annas, a rupee or more, pile up to fifty or sixty rupees in the end. They all say, "I'll just come and pay the amount", but don't do so even in two months' time... Oh, is that you, Mr. Banerji? When did you get back? Please accept my obeisance.'

Banerji had a brass pot in his left hand. Mud clung to his toe-nails and heels. His sacred thread was wound around his ear and in his right hand he clutched some shrimps wrapped in a leaf. He breathed out noisily, with a hiss, and answered, 'I returned last night. Now, Madhu, pass me a smoke, will you?' He then placed his pot on the ground and opened the packet of shrimps in his hand. 'Can you imagine, Madhu, how Sairubi the fisherwoman behaved with me? She had the audacity to grab my hands! How the times have changed! And is this

40

small quantity of shrimps worth one pice? But how long can that slut go on cheating a Brahmin? Won't she come to great grief?'

Madhu expressed his surprise and said, 'What! She grabbed your hands!'

The furious Mr. Banerji looked around and spoke excitedly, 'I owed her only two and a half pice. Is that any reason why she should grab my hands in the marketplace in the presence of so many people! Who hasn't seen it, eh? I had relieved myself in the fields and gone to the river to wash my hands and feet. There I thought I might as well take a round of the marketplace before returning home. The slut was there with a basketful of shrimps. But she told me that there was nothing left... everything had been sold out. She thought she'd fool me, eh? All of a sudden I pulled the lid off the basket and saw... She too thrust out her hand and caught hold of my wrist! Maybe I owe her three and a half pice–the two-and-a-half I owed her before and now one pice for these. But am I running away from this village just to avoid payment of this paltry sum? What d'you say, Madhu?'

Madhu agreed, 'Is that at all possible?'

'You have said it. Is there any discipline in this village? Had there been any, her husband, that fisherman Shashthi, would've been an outcaste by now with the services of the barber and the washerman denied to him, his thatched roof cut, and they would have been run out of the village.'

Suddenly his eyes fell on Ramesh. 'Who's this gentleman, Madhu?'

'Why, he is the son of our Tarini Babu,' replied Madhu, proudly. 'He has come all the way to pay up the balance of ten rupees which was due to me.'

Mr. Banerji forgot his complaint about the shrimps. With his eyes wide with surprise, he exclaimed, 'Who? Dear Ramesh? May you live long! I heard, on my return

home, that you had really done a job of the funeral ceremony of your father, that such a feast had never been
given in these parts before. What a pity I couldn't see it
with my own eyes! At the suggestion of some bluffers I
went to Calcutta in search of a job and had to suffer the
lot of a sweeper. What an awful place, Calcutta! Can
anyone stay there? '

Ramesh looked silently at his face, but the others
present in the shop were eager to hear Banerji's story
about his visit to Calcutta. Madhu handed over the
hookah to him and asked, 'Why, what happened? Could
you get a job? '

'Why not? Did I have my education for nothing? But
it was of no use. It's impossible to stay in Calcutta.
There's as much smoke as mud there. If you go out on
business and can manage to return home without being
run over by cars and carriages, you should account it to
your inherited merit.'

Madhu had never been to Calcutta himself. He had
only once gone to Midnapore to give evidence in a case.
He was greatly surprised and said, 'You don't say!'

Banerji smiled a little, 'Ask your Ramesh Babu
whether this is true or not. No, Madhu, I'd rather starve
at home but I'll never go to Calcutta again. You won't
believe it, one has to buy even such worthless things as
sour-apples, hog-plums, banana-flowers and banana-
stems there! Can you afford to spend money on such
trash? Within this one month I've become as thin as a
church-mouse. Besides, my stomach rumbled and chest
burned all the time. Life became miserable! In the end
I had to run away to save my life. Even if I've only one
meal a day at home, I won't mind it. If necessary, I'd beg.
A Brahmin needn't be ashamed of begging. I'll let
Mother Lakshmi, the goddess of Fortune, be... but never
again shall I leave the village!'

Banerji's story had shocked everyone into silence. He
now stood up and going near the oil jar, poured out a

measure of oil with a ladle into his left palm. Half of this he dropped in his nostrils and ears, and rubbed his hair with the rest. 'It's getting late. I'd better take a dip in the river before going home. Madhu, let me have one pice worth of salt. I'll pay you in the afternoon.'

'Again in the afternoon!' moaned Madhu. He went inside the shop with a sour look on his face. Banerji craned his neck and said, in a voice full of surprise and annoyance, 'What's the matter with you people?... Have you all become cutthroats? It's as good as extortion!' He then advanced and took out a large handful of salt, put it in a paper bag and picking up the pot, said to Ramesh with a grin, 'We'll be going the same way. Let's get going, Son. We can then chat on the way.'

'All right', said Ramesh, and stood up.

Standing at a distance, Madhu said, mournfully, 'Mr. Banerji... the five annas due for the flour – would you at the same time ...'

Banerji flew into a rage and exclaimed, 'Hey, Madhu, we'll be seeing each other twice a day now that I'm here... have you no shame left in you? I've just had to spend as much as five rupees in travel to Calcutta, at the suggestion of some rascals. Is this the time for you to start pressing for repayment of dues! As they say, what's sport to the cat is death to the rat! Really, Ramesh, you see how these people behave!'

Embarrassed, Madhu mumbled, 'It's long since...'

'What of that? If all of you start harassing me like this, I can't possibly continue to live in this village.'

Clutching at his things, Banerji left in a huff.

As Ramesh entered his house, a gentleman, who was sitting there, hastily got up and, pushing his *hookah* to one side, did obeisance to Ramesh at his feet. Rising he said, 'I'm Banamali Parui, Headmaster of the village school. I came twice, but couldn't meet you, so I thought...'

Ramesh received him warmly and offered him a chair. But Mr. Parui remained standing, respectfully. 'Your servant, Sir,' he said in protestation.

He was an old man and was, besides, a teacher in the school. His excessive humility and cringing behaviour evoked disrespect in Ramesh. Parui could not be persuaded to sit on the chair. He remained standing while he narrated the story of the school.

'It is a small school, but the only one of its kind in this locality. It was founded by the Mukharjis and the Ghoshals. About thirty or forty students attend this school. Some come from a distance of even five or six miles. The school also receives a small grant from the government. Yet it has become increasingly difficult to run it any longer.'

Ramesh remembered that he too had attended this school for some time in his childhood. Parui informed Ramesh that unless the roof was rethatched before the rains, it would not be possible for anyone to sit inside the rooms during the coming monsoon. But even that could wait a bit longer. The immediate worry was non-payment of the salary of the teachers. None of them had been paid for the last three months, and they were not prepared to work any longer for nothing.

The story about the school aroused Ramesh's interest. He took the Headmaster to the sitting room and collected from him all the information regarding the school. Parui added that the school had four teachers. Through their efforts, on an average, two students passed the Middle English examination every year. Here Parui recited their names and addresses as if he had got them by heart. The salary of the two juniormost teachers was somehow met from the school fees. The government grants covered the salary of another teacher, but that of the remaining one teacher was met from donations raised in and around the village. This responsibility rested with the teachers. But although

44

they had made a round of each house eight or ten times already, they had not been able to raise more than seven rupees and four annas.

Ramesh was stunned. This was the only school in all these five or six villages, yet it had not been possible to raise more than seven rupees and four annas in spite of repeated attempts during the last three or four months!

Ramesh questioned him, 'How much do you get?'

'I have to sign a receipt for twenty-six rupees, but actually I get only thirteen rupees and fifteen annas.'

Ramesh was unable to comprehend what he had said and continued to stare at him. The teacher understood the meaning of that look and explained, 'Sir, according to government orders, a receipt for twenty-six rupees has to be shown to the Sub-Inspector of Schools. Otherwise the government grant would be stopped. Everybody knows this. You may ask any student and find out that I'm not telling a lie.'

Ramesh remained silent for a long time and then said, 'But doesn't that mean you lose face among the students?'

The Headmaster was abashed, 'What can I do, Ramesh Babu? Beni Babu isn't ready even to pay this small amount.'

'Oh, he's the boss, is he?'

The Headmaster hesitated for a moment, but the matter was urgent. So he began, slowly, 'He's the Secretary all right. But he never spends even a single pice from his own pocket. But for the generosity of Jadu Mukharji's daughter – she is Goddess Lakshmi herself – but for her this school would've closed down long ago. She had given us hope that she'd take care of the entire expenses for the thatching this year. But for some unknown reason she has suddenly stopped all help.'

Ramesh became curious. He made some more queries regarding Rama and in the end, asked, 'Isn't her brother a student of your school?'

'You mean Jatin? Yes, he is.'

Ramesh said, 'It's getting late for your school. I shouldn't delay you further. I'll come round and see you tomorrow.'

'All right, sir', said the Headmaster and made another obeisance to Ramesh, and insisted on taking the dust from his feet and placing it on his head, before he left.

CHAPTER
6

The story of what Bishweshwari did on the day of the funerary ceremony spread through the length and breadth of ten neighbouring villages the very same day. By nature, Beni was incapable of speaking rudely to anyone's face. So he went and fetched Rama's aunt. It is said that in ancient times Takshak, the great mythical serpent, once bit a huge Asvattha tree (*Ficus religiosa*) and its poison burnt the tree to ashes. The poison which Rama's aunt spread with her tongue that morning, attacking Bishweshwari in her own home, was no less powerful; though it did not turn Bishweshwari into ashes, either because her body was of flesh and blood, and not of wood, or because the present age was different from the past. Bishweshwari swallowed all the insults silently. She knew very well that the woman was acting at the instigation of her own son. But she was afraid that if she retorted, the woman would give out the fact of her son's involvement, which, if it reached Ramesh's ears, would cause her greater humiliation. So she remained silent all through.

But nothing remains a secret in the countryside. Ramesh came to hear about the incident. From the very beginning he was greatly worried about Aunty. He had also apprehended that the incident involving Sukumari might lead to a difference between the mother and the son. But he had never dreamt that Beni would go to the length of engaging an outsider to insult and torment his own mother. It was totally immaterial. The thought made his blood boil and his very being blazed with indig-

47

nation. His first impulse was to rush to Beni's house and abuse him roundly. He felt that a man, who could be so mean as to insult his own mother in this manner, deserved no consideration. But on second thoughts it occurred to him that it would aggravate Aunty's insult and not abate it; so he must refrain from that.

From what he had heard about Rama, first from Dinu the other day and then from the Headmaster, Ramesh had developed a genuine esteem for her. He had earlier been convinced that in the midst of all the stupidity and contemptible meanness of the people in this village, Aunty with her largeness of heart was the only beacon light of hope; everything else was steeped in darkness. Then he felt that another light – however small and dim – burnt within the Mukharji home, and this feeling had given him great satisfaction.

But now this incident of Aunty's insult by Rama's aunt once more filled his heart with hatred and disgust against Rama. He had not the least doubt in his mind that these two women, Rama and her aunt, had committed this grave offence in collusion with Beni. But he was unable to think of a possible way of punishing Beni or of taking suitable action against these two women.

Just at that time something happened. Some of their properties were still held jointly by the Mukharjis and the Ghoshals. The pond known as 'Garh', behind the Acharjya house, was one such joint possession. At one time it had been a fairly large tank, but it had shrunk for want of proper renovation, and was now no more than a ditch. Good varieties of spawn were not reared in it. So it had no good fish in it. Only ordinary and common varieties like *koi* and *magur*, which grow in muddy ditches, were to be found there.

One morning Bhairab came running and panting. Ramesh's steward, Gopal Sarkar, was making entries in his account books in a room adjacent to the House of Worship. Bhairab said hastily, 'Mr. Sarkar, they're casting their net in the "Garh" for fish. Haven't you sent your men yet?'

Sarkar tucked his pen behind his ears and looked up at Bhairab, 'Who's ordered the catch?'

'Who else? Beni Babu's servant is there. The up-country watchman of the Mukharjis is also there. Only there's none from your side. Send a man immediately.'

Gopal was not in the least ruffled. He simply said, 'Our Babu doesn't take fish or meat.'

'He may not, but surely you ought to claim your share.'

'Thus you and I think,' said Gopal. 'And if my old master were alive today, he would also have thought so. But Ramesh Babu is a man of different temperament.' Noticing a surprised look on Bhairab's face, he added sourly, 'This is after all a very small matter... Just a question of a few *magur* and *singi* fish, Mr. Acharjya. Only the other day they felled the huge tamarind tree on the northern side of the market and divided the wood between their two houses and didn't give us even a stick. When I heard of it, I came running and informed my master. He simply lifted his eyes from the book he was reading, smiled, and continued reading. I asked, "Shouldn't we do something, Sir?"

'This time our Ramesh Babu hadn't time even to look up at me. When I pressed hard, he closed the book, yawned and then said, "Wood? Aren't there other tamarind trees?" Have you ever heard of such a thing! I said, "Of course there are! But why should we forgo our due share? And whoever does that?" Ramesh Babu held the book open and kept quiet for about five minutes. He then said, "That's right, but one can't afford to fight over a few pieces of firewood!" '

Bhairab was greatly astonished 'Really?'

Gopal Sarkar shook his head once or twice and smiled. 'What I say is true, Mr. Acharjya, it's true! I was convinced that very day that the Goddess of Fortune had indeed deserted this house with the death of Tarini Ghoshal. Then, why bother?'

Bhairab remained silent for a while and then said, 'But the water-tank is just behind my house... I must at least inform him once.'

Gopal replied, 'Very well, Sir, why don't you go and tell him yourself? If a landowner remains busy all the time with books and is scared of his co-sharers, how can he preserve his property? They say even Jadu Mukharji's daughter – a woman, mind you – rolled with laughter at this! I'm told that she sent for Govinda Ganguly the other day and said jokingly, "Why don't you ask Ramesh Babu to hand over his estate to me and be satisfied with a monthly pension?" What can be more humiliating than this?' With a face distraught with anger and sorrow, Gopal started minding his account books.

There was no woman in the house. So everyone had free access into it. On entering, Bhairab found Ramesh reclining on a broken easy chair in the front verandah. In order to incite Ramesh to his duty, Bhairab made some preliminary remarks about the need for preservation of one's property and then raised the question of the catch of fish. Ramesh immediately gave a roar like a sleeping tiger hit by a bullet. 'What! Playing tricks every day! Bhajua!'

This inconceivable and completely unexpected outburst from Ramesh unnerved Bhairab. He was not sure who was playing tricks. Bhajua was Ramesh's servant from Gorakhpur district. He was exceptionally strong and reliable. He was Ramesh's disciple in the art of fighting with bamboo staves. After learning it himself, Ramesh had trained Bhajua. As soon as Bhajua appeared before him, Ramesh gave him clear orders. 'Go and bring all the fish here! If anybody tries to stop you, drag him along to this place by his hair. If it isn't possible to do that, at least break one set of his teeth!'

This was exactly what Bhajua wanted. Without a word he went back to his room to fetch his long stave – hardened by constant rubbing of oil.

This completely terrified Bhairab. He was a soft Bengali gentleman, not at all afraid of shouts. But the sight of the strongly built, short-statured up-country man, who did not utter a single word but simply nodded and went away, was too much for his nerves and he lost them completely. He remembered that the dog that does not bark is sure to bite. Bhairab was a real well-wisher of Ramesh. So he had come to inform him and also to suggest that if Ramesh sent someone to the spot in time with instructions to hurl abuses, if necessary, he would be able to get his share of the fish. Bhairab was himself prepared to help him, if necessary. But nothing like that happened. Nobody seemed to be in favour of shouting and abusing. The master at least gave a roar, but the servant did not even open his lips. He straightaway went off to bring his stave. Now Bhairab was a poor man; he had neither the courage nor the intention to be implicated in a criminal case. After a while Bhajua reappeared with his long bamboo stave, saluted Ramesh from a distance by touching his forehead with the stave and was on the point of leaving. All on a sudden Bhairab burst into tears and clasping both of Ramesh's hands, cried, 'O Bhajua, for heaven's sake, don't go! Ramesh, my son, please spare me. I'm a poor man. This'll mean death to me!'

Ramesh was annoyed, and freed his hands. His surprise knew no bounds. Bhajua came back and stood perplexed. Bhairab sobbed, 'This won't remain a secret. Once Beni Babu hears of this, I'll be completely ruined. My life will be in danger, and even my house will be set on fire. Nobody will be able to save me from his clutches – not even Brahma and Vishnu!'

Ramesh hung down his head and remained seated like one stunned.

Attracted by the noise, Gopal Sarkar had come over there from his work. He now said softly, 'What he says is true, Sir.'

Ramesh gave no answer but simply waved Bhajua away to go about with his own work. He then got up and without a word entered his room. Bhairab Acharjya's excessive fear and piteous cries raged through his heart like a tempest – God alone knew what was passing through his mind!

CHAPTER
7

'How's it, Jatin, you're still playing? Won't you go to school today?'

'No, Didi, our school's closed today and tomorrow.'

Rama's aunt heard this and remarked with a scowl, which made her ugly face look uglier. 'What a worthless school! It remains closed for at least fifteen days in a month! And you go on spending money on such a school! Had I been in your place, I'd have set it on fire!' Saying this she went about her own work.

Those who spoke ill of the aunt on the ground that she was a complete liar and never deviated from it to speak the truth, were wrong. Once in a while she could speak the truth, as on this occasion, and if necessary, follow it up with action.

Rama drew her younger brother closer to her and lowering her voice, asked, 'Why is the school closed, Jatin?'

Jatin nestled in her sister's lap, and replied, 'The roof is being thatched, that's why. Afterwards the walls will be whitewashed. Lots of books and furniture – four or five chairs and tables, a cupboard, a very large clock – all these have arrived. Why don't you go one day and see all these things, Didi?'

Rama was greatly surprised. 'You don't say!'

'It's true, Didi. Ramesh Babu who has come is getting all these done.'

The boy was going to say something more, but noticing that her aunt was coming that way, Rama took Jatin to her own room. She lovingly made him sit by her side and with a series of questions came to know all that Ramesh was doing for the school. She also learnt that Ramesh himself took classes for one or two hours every day. All on a sudden she asked, 'Does he recognize you, Jatin?'

'Oh, yes,' replied Jatin, proudly nodding.

'How do you call him?'

Poor Jatin was now in a fix. So far he had not had the privilege or courage to have personal acquaintance with Ramesh. As soon as Ramesh appeared, even the mighty Headmaster became nervous. This excited fear and amazement in the students to such an extent that they did not even dare to look Ramesh in the face, not to speak of addressing him. But it was not possible for Jatin to acknowledge this before his elder sister. He had heard that the teachers addressed Ramesh as 'Chhoto Babu', the young Master. So he made the best possible use of his intelligence and said, 'Why, we call him "Chhoto Babu".' But Rama was able to know from his countenance that this was not true.

She drew him closer to her and said, smilingly, 'Why "Chhoto Babu"? He's an elder brother to you. As you call Beni Babu "Dada", so you may call him the same.'

The boy became restless with surprise and delight. 'Is he really an elder brother to me? Are you speaking the truth, Didi?'

'Of course', said Rama, with another smile.

It now became difficult to hold Jatin back any longer. He was anxious to run away and spread this precious piece of news among his schoolmates. But the school was closed for two days; somehow he had to be patient for these two days. However there were some boys who lived near by. How could he not tell them at once! He became restless and said, 'May I go now, Didi?'

'It's so late, where'll you go in the sun now?' said Rama, holding him back. Unable to go, Jatin became unhappy and remained silent for some time. He then asked, 'Where was he all this time, Didi?'

Rama replied, gently, 'He was studying abroad. When you grow older, you too will have to go somewhere for your studies. Will you be able to stay away from me?'

She drew him closer to her bosom. Although he was still a small boy, Jatin perceived a change in his sister's voice and looked up at her face in surprise. Though Rama loved her brother more than her own life, never before had she expressed such emotion in her talk or behaviour.

Jatin asked, 'Has Ramesh-da finished his studies, Didi?' Rama replied, affectionately, 'Yes, he has.'

Jatin next asked, 'How do you know?'

In reply Rama simply nodded and sighed. As a matter of fact, neither she nor anyone else in the village had any definite information on this point. She was not sure that her guess was correct either. But somehow she felt that one who took so much interest in the education of other people's children could not be an uneducated person himself.

Jatin did not press for an answer to his question, because a new question had in the mean time struck his mind. He now asked, abruptly, 'Well, Didi, why doesn't Ramesh-da come to our house? Dada comes everyday.'

This question gave Rama a shock like a sudden spasm of acute pain. Yet she said, smilingly, 'Can't you request him to come?'

Jatin jumped up immediately and said, 'Shall I go now, Didi?'

'Oh, what a mad boy you are!' she said and then hurriedly hugged him hard, overcome by fear and anxiety. 'No, no, Jatin, you must never do that, never!' she said and held him close to her with all her might. Jatin clearly perceived the quick throbbing of her heart and, though a child himself, he was filled with awe and gazed silently at her face. He had never seen his sister behave like this before and now that he knew that the venerable Chhoto Babu was his own Ramesh-da, and his thought had turned to a completely different direction, he failed to understand why his sister should be so very afraid.

Rama now heard the shrill voice of her aunt. She hastily released Jatin and rose to her feet. Almost immediately Aunt came there and stood at the door. 'I was under the impression that you had gone to the pond for your bath. Today may be your day of fast, but does that mean that you shouldn't even take your bath till one o'clock? You look so dark and haggard!'

Rama forced a smile on her lips and said, 'You go ahead Aunt, I'll follow.'

'How will you go now? Just come out and see... Beni and the others have come to divide the fish.'

At the mention of the word 'fish' Jatin scampered away. Rama cleaned her face by rubbing it hard with the border of her sari, unnoticed by her aunt, and followed her into the courtyard.

There was a lot of noise in the courtyard. The quantity of fish was not small – almost one large basketful. Beni had come personally to take his share of the catch. All the children of the neighbourhood had assembled there; they had come with the basket of fish and were making a rumpus around it.

A cough was heard and the next moment appeared Dharmadas with his walking stick in hand. 'How was the catch, Beni?' he asked.

'Nothing worth mention,' said Beni, with a look of displeasure. He then told the fisherman, 'Why delay? Why don't you divide the catch quickly into two equal shares?' The fisherman started his work.

'How d'you do, Rama? I wasn't able to come and see you for quite some time. So I thought of coming over,' said Govinda Ganguly, as he entered the house.

'Please come in,' said Rama. An amused smile played

lightly in the corners of her mouth.

'What's this crowd about?' enquired Govinda as he advanced towards the spot. All on a sudden he seemed to be completely taken by surprise. 'Oh, I see. Quite a nice catch of fish! Was the catch made in the large pond?'

Nobody thought it necessary to give any reply to these questions. They were all attention to the fisherman's work of dividing the fish. Soon that work was over..Beni placed almost the entire quantity of his share into a basket, and made his servant carry it on his head. He winked at the fisherman and turned to go. As the need of the Mukharji family was little, a good portion of Rama's share was distributed among the gentlemen present according to their importance, and they were also on the point of leaving for their homes.

Suddenly, they were all startled to see that the short-statured up-country servant of Ramesh Ghoshal had come and taken his stand right in the middle of the courtyard, carrying with him a long bamboo stave almost equal to his height. The man had such a forbidding appearance that wherever he went, he immediately caught everybody's eyes and whoever saw him once remembered him for ever. Everyone in the village, old and young, knew him. In fact some strange stories about him circulated in the village and were coming to be accepted as true. How he could single out Rama as the mistress of the house from among all these people was known only to him. However, he saluted her from a distance, addressed her as 'Mother', and came nearer. Whatever might be his appearance, his voice was really fierce – very hoarse and cracked. He saluted her again and spoke in a mixture of Hindi and Bengali. He said briefly that he was Ramesh Babu's servant and had come to take his master's one-third share of the catch. Rama was unable to give any prompt answer – either because of her bewilderment at the turn of events or her inability to know how to refute this reasonable request.

The man suddenly turned round, looked at Beni's servant and said, gruffly, 'Hey, don't go!'

The servant hurriedly retreated a few steps. There was total silence for half a minute and then Beni made bold to ask, from where he was standing, 'What share?'

Bhajua immediately saluted him and said respectfully, 'Sir, I haven't spoken to you.'

Rama's aunt, who was standing on an open porch at a distance, said in a shrill, clattering voice, 'What! Are you going to beat us?'

Bhajua looked at her for a moment and then burst into a loud and harsh guffaw, which reverberated through the whole house. Soon he checked his laughter, rather ashamed, and looking at Rama with an inquiring look said, 'Well, Mother?'

Somehow Rama imagined that there was contempt hidden behind all this facade of respectful talk and courteous behaviour which the man showed her. This irritated her. 'What does your master want?' she now asked.

Bhajua noticed Rama's annoyance and was embarrassed. So he made his harsh voice as gentle as possible and repeated his request. But what could Rama do? The fish had already been divided and distributed. Moreover, she could not afford to look small in the presence of so many persons. So she said rudely, 'Your master hasn't any share in it. Go and tell him. Let him do what he can!'

'Very well, Mother,' said Bhajua, and made a respectful bow. He then waved Beni's servant away and without another word turned to go.

When all the people present were struck with amazement at his behaviour, he suddenly turned back and addressing Rama in his usual mixture of Hindi and Bengali, begged her pardon for his harsh voice and said, 'Mother, having heard about it from others my master had ordered me to come to the pond and take away all the fish by force. Neither he nor I take fish or meat, but...' He added, with a slap on his broad chest with his right hand, 'If necessary, I was prepared to lay down my life at the edge of that pond to carry out my master's orders; but Lord Rama saved the situation. After some time my master's anger abated. Calling me, he said, "Bhajua, go and ask the young Mistress whether I've any share in that pond"'. He then raised his two hands holding the stave towards Rama and touched his head with them in a profound salutation, and continued, 'Master said, "Whatever others may say, I know for certain that the young Mistress will never tell a lie and will never touch anybody else's things."' Saluting her repeatedly in a most respectful manner he went away.

As soon as Bhajua had left, Beni started, boastfully, in a shrill emasculated voice, 'Oh, this is how he's going to preserve his estate! I swear in the presence of you all that henceforth I won't allow him to touch even a snail or a shellfish from the pond. Mark it, Rama.' Beni was beside himself with joy and went on cackling for some time.

Not a word of what Beni said entered Rama's ears. Bhajua's words – 'the young Mistress will never tell a lie – echoing and re-echoing through her ears like the clapping of a million hands seemed to tear through her head. Her fair face became crimson for a moment and then turned deathly pale, as if drained of the last drop of blood. Rama was insensible to everything else except the thought that nobody should see her face in this condition. So she hastily covered her face with the border of her sari and disappeared into the house.

CHAPTER
8

'Aunty!'

'Is that you, Ramesh? Come, my boy, come in.' Bishweshwari quickly spread a rush mat on the floor for Ramesh to sit.

As soon as Ramesh stepped into the room, he was startled. Though he could not see her face, it was clear to him that the woman sitting near Aunty was Rama. He said to himself, with a good deal of irritation, that this lady, who had no hesitation in insulting Aunty through her aunt, could be shameless enough to come and sit by her side in seclusion.

On the other hand, Ramesh's sudden arrival caused no less embarrassment to Rama. Not only was she born and brought up in this village, but her relation with Ramesh was such that she could not possibly cover her face and turn aside as to a stranger, nor could she feel at ease without a veil. Besides, there was that incident about the fish the other day. So in order to avoid awkwardness as much as possible, she sat and looked away as if to avoid him. Ramesh did not glance at her again either. He completely ignored the presence of a third person in the room and settled down on the mat.

'Aunty!'

'Yes, my boy. What made you come at this hour of mid-afternoon?'

'Because unless I come at noon I don't get an opportunity to sit with you for some time. You always seem to be so busy!'

Aunty said nothing to contradict him, but simply smiled.

Ramesh continued with a wan smile. 'Aunty, many years ago when I was a child, I once took leave of you. I've come to do so once again. This may very well be the last time.' In spite of the smile on his face, his voice indicated great sadness and depression which struck both Aunty and Rama with painful surprise.

'Oh, no, my child! Don't say that. May Goddess Shasthi give you a long life!' Bishweshwari's eyes were suffused with tears.

Ramesh said nothing, but simply smiled.

Bishweshwari asked affectionately, 'Aren't you well here, my son?'

Ramesh cast a glance at his own tall and very strong body once or twice, and then said, 'I'm all right, Aunty. This body which was nourished with up-country food, like *dal* and *roti*, doesn't give way so easily. No, I'm quite well so far as health is concerned. But I can't continue to live here even for a moment. I feel suffocated from time to time.'

Reassured that Ramesh was not unwell, Bishweshwari said with a smile, 'You were born here. Weren't you? Then how is it that you can't survive here?'

Ramesh shook his head. 'I don't want to say anything about it. I'm sure you know everything.'

Bishweshwari remained silent for a while and then said, gravely, 'Well, I may not know everything, but I know at least some of it. That's exactly the reason why I say it won't do if you go away to some other place, Ramesh.'

'Why not, Aunty? Nobody wants me here.'

'That's just the reason why I won't allow you to run away from this place. Just now you boasted of your dal-and-roti-fed body. Is it meant for running away?'

Ramesh remained silent. There was a special reason why his mind had revolted against the entire village that

61

day. A portion of the road running from the village to the railway station had been washed away by floods some eight or ten years ago. The breach had since become wider and deeper. Some water almost always accumulated there. Crossing that bit was a matter of anxiety for everyone. At other times people somehow crossed the place very cautiously, on tiptoe and by lifting their cloths; but during the rainy months there was no end of difficulty. Sometimes a few bamboo poles were placed over the breach, or a broken palmyra canoe was placed upside down across it. With its help people somehow crossed the breach; and in doing so, sometimes some of them fell down and even broke their limbs. Yet, in spite of all these difficulties, the villagers had done nothing to repair the breach. The work was likely to cost only twenty rupees or so. Instead of meeting the entire expenses himself, Ramesh had tried to raise public subscription for this purpose. But he was not able to raise even eight or ten pice on all these eight or ten days. What added insult to injury was the conversation in a goldsmith's shop, which he overheard while returning from his walk that morning. One was telling another with a laugh, 'Don't give a single pice, any of you. Don't you see that his own necessity is the greatest?... He wants to go along the road with his shoes squeaking; if you don't pay anything, he'll get the work done at his own cost. Well, when he wasn't here, didn't we get to the railway station?'

Someone else remarked, 'Just you wait and see! Mr. Chatterjee was telling us that they were trying to get the temple of Goddess Shitala repaired at his cost. One has only to coax and flatter him a bit!' Since then, the whole morning, this talk had been rankling in his heart; it seemed to burn him, as it were.

Bishweshwari hit him exactly at this sensitive spot. 'You were trying to get that breach repaired ... what happened to it?' she asked.

Ramesh felt annoyed, 'That can't be done, Aunty. Nobody is prepared to give even a single pice for it.'

Bishweshwari smiled. 'Is that enough for you to give up the idea? You've inherited a large sum of money from your grandfather, haven't you? You can very well pay this small amount yourself.'

Ramesh was inflamed. 'But why should I? I regret that I was foolish enough to spend so much money on their school. One shouldn't do anything for this village!' He looked at Rama through the corners of his eyes, and added, 'If you give to charity, they take you to be a fool. If you do good to them, they assume that you must've some interest in it. Even forgiving is a fault – they think you've backed out from fear!'

Aunty burst out laughing; but Rama turned crimson. Ramesh demanded, angrily, 'Why did you laugh, Aunty?'

'I couldn't help it, my boy.' She then heaved a sigh, and added, 'But I think that's all the more reason why you should stay here. If you're thinking of leaving your birthplace just because you're angry with them, I say, is there anyone here worthy of your anger?' After a pause, she said, as if to herself, 'You don't know, Ramesh, how miserable and helpless these people are! Had you known, you'd have been ashamed of yourself for being angry with such people. If God has so kindly sent you here.... do remain here in their midst, my boy.'

'But none of them wants me here, Aunty.'

'Doesn't it explain to you how very unworthy they are of your anger? Not only these people... go to any village you like, you'll see the same everywhere.'

Suddenly her eyes fell on Rama. 'What's the matter with you, dear? You've been sitting with your head hanging down all this while. Ramesh, aren't you two – brother and sister – on speaking terms? Rama, my dear, that isn't right. Whatever misunderstanding you might have had with his father should have ended with his death. It won't do if you two continue to nurse the old misunderstanding.'

Rama said mildly with downcast eyes, 'I don't want to continue the misunderstanding, Aunty. Ramesh-da...'

But her soft voice was hushed by Ramesh's angry and grave tone. He got up and said, 'Aunty, please don't get yourself involved in this. You've somehow survived the attack from her aunt the other day. If she now goes and sends her aunt again today, she'll eat you up alive before returning home.' With these words Ramesh left the room hurriedly, without waiting for any protests.

Bishweshwari shouted after him. 'Don't go, Ramesh! Listen to what I say!'

Ramesh replied from outside the door, 'No, Aunty. Don't you speak a word on behalf of those who, in their insolence and pride, don't hesitate even to trample you under their feet!' Before Aunty could make a second request, Ramesh was already gone.

Completely bewildered, Rama continued to stare at Bishweshwari's face for a few moments and then suddenly burst into tears. 'Why this accusation against me, Aunty? Do I tutor my aunt that I should be held responsible for her conduct?'

Aunty drew Rama's hand into her own and said affectionately, 'It's true that you don't tutor your aunt; but you can't possibly avoid some responsibility for her conduct.'

Wiping her tears away with her other hand Rama vehemently contradicted Aunty in a voice full of suppressed anger and pride, 'Why should I be held responsible? Certainly not! I didn't even have an inkling of that affair. Why did he have to accuse me falsely and insult me?'

Bishweshwari did not prolong the controversy. She said gently, 'Everyone can't be expected to know the inside story. But I can assure you that he hadn't the least intention of insulting you. You don't know, Rama, but

I've heard from Gopal Sarkar how great is his regard for you and how deep is his faith in you. The other day when the tamarind tree was cut and the firewood shared between the two families, he didn't listen to anyone who said that he too had a share in it. He laughed at them and said, "There's absolutely no reason for me to worry. So long as Rama's there, I'll certainly get my due share; she'll never misappropriate someone else's things." I know very well that even after all the unpleasantness, he had the fullest faith in you until that incident of the fish pond the other day...'

In the midst of her talk Bishweshwari suddenly stopped and continued staring at Rama's pale and downcast face for some time. At last she said, 'I'd like to tell you one thing today, my dear. However important it may be for you to preserve your estate, Ramesh's life is much more important than all that. You mustn't destroy it by repeated blows from all sides, at the instigation of anyone or for the sake of anything. It'll mean irreparable loss to this village. I'm sure you won't be able to make up that loss by any means.'

Rama kept quiet. She did not say even a word to contradict Aunty. Bishweshwari also did not say anything more. After some time Rama said, almost inaudibly, 'It's getting late, Aunty. I must be going now.' She bowed down and taking the dust from Aunty's feet, left.

CHAPTER
9

However angry Ramesh might have been when he left, his anger was gone by the time he reached home. He said to himself again and again, 'Strange that I didn't understand this simple thing and suffered so miserably! In fact, with whom should I be angry? These people are so narrow-minded and selfish that they don't even understand what's really good for them. Lack of education has made them so blind that they think the weakening of their neighbour is the best way of strengthening themselves. If one does them a good turn, they immediately become suspicious. Nothing could be more foolish than being angry with such people.'

He remembered how in that far-off city he had formed an impression of these Bengal villages by reading books and hearing stories about them, and by imagining things. He had believed that if the Bengalis had nothing else, they had at least peace and happiness in their villages which were absent in the populous cities. There the simple and contented villagers were full of sympathy for their neighbours. When someone was in distress, others came forward to offer their help. When someone was rejoicing, others came uninvited to share in his happiness. It was only there, in those sympathetic hearts, that the real wealth of the Bengalis was still to be found intact. But alas, what a grave mistake! He had never come across such disputes and jealousies even in towns. Whenever he had noticed some sign of a sinful act in the busy streets of the city he had always thought that once he was able to go back to the small village which was his birthplace, he would be spared those ugly sights once and for all. He had believed that the villagers still retained their most precious possession, namely, religion, and that the social character was still unimpaired there. But O God! Where's that character? Where's that living religion in our old, sequestered villages? If religion is devoid of life, what is the use of the corpse which is left behind? The unfortunate members of the village community are clinging with all their might to this disfigured and discoloured corpse as the thing itself and its poisonous and cadaverous slipperiness is sending them day and night into the abyss. But the heart-rending irony is that, it is these villagers again who regard the townspeople as men without religion and caste and treat them with so much contempt and disregard!

As soon as Ramesh entered the house, he found an elderly woman and a boy aged about eleven or twelve huddled together in one corner of the courtyard. Seeing him they stood up. Even though he knew nothing about them, the face of the boy touched his heart. Gopal Sarkar, who was writing something, came over from the porch adjacent to the House of Prayer and said, 'This boy is the son of Dwarik Thakur of the southern part of the village. He has come to you to beg for help'.

At the mention of the word 'beg', Ramesh flared up. 'Have I come home, Mr. Sarkar, only to give alms to others? Is there none else in this village?'

Gopal Sarkar was a bit embarrassed. 'That's of course true, Sir,' he said. 'But the old Master never denied help to anyone. That's why whenever one is in difficulty, he comes running to this house.' He glanced at the boy, and then spoke to the elderly woman. 'Well, Kamini's mother, these people are also to blame. So long as Dwarik Thakur lived, they didn't arrange for the expiatory rites, and now that nobody comes forward to carry

67

the body, they come knocking at the door, begging for money. Aren't there even pots and pans in the house?'

Kamini's mother was a Sadgop (farmer) by caste and was a neighbour of the boy. She shook her head and said, 'If you don't believe me, come and see for yourself. If I had anything left, I wouldn't have brought him along to beg, with the body lying around. You might not have seen, but you must have heard how I maintained this poor family for the last six months with all that I owned. How could I allow a Brahmin family living next door to die of starvation?'

Ramesh was able to guess to some extent what the matter was. Gopal Sarkar elaborated on it. 'This boy's father, Dwarik Chakraborty, who had been suffering from consumption for the last six months, died this morning. Nobody is coming forward to touch the corpse because the prescribed expiatory rites weren't performed before Dwarik's death. Kamini's mother has exhausted all her resources on this poor Brahmin family in the last six months. She too has nothing more left. So she has come to you with this boy.'

Ramesh remained silent for a while and then said, 'It's almost two o'clock now. Will the body remain where it is until the expiatory rites are performed?'

Gopal Sarkar smiled and said, 'That can't be helped, Sir. Nothing can be done in contravention of the laws of the sacred books. And who can blame the neighbours either? However, the corpse can't remain like that ... they'll have to arrange for the prescribed rites somehow. That's why they're begging. But Kamini's mother, did you go to anyone else?'

The boy opened his fist and showed a four-anna piece and four pice. Kamini's mother said, 'The Mukharjis have given the four-anna piece, and Mr. Haldar has given those four pice. But, in any case, anything less than two rupees and four annas won't do. So if Babu will please...'

Ramesh said hurriedly, 'You may go home now! You needn't go to any other place. I'll send my man over immediately for arranging everything.' After seeing them off, Ramesh looked at Gopal Sarkar with sorrowful eyes and asked, 'Do you know how many such poor families are there in this village?'

'Not many, Sir... only two or three', replied Sarkar. 'They also had some landed property and were able to live somehow on coarse rice and cloth, but prolonged litigation over an ordinary Chalta tree between Dwarik Chakrabarty and Sanatan Hajra about five years ago completely ruined them both.' He then lowered his voive and added, 'Matters wouldn't have gone that far, but our Beni Babu and Govinda Ganguly fanned the fire.'

'Then?'

'Then whatever property the two families had was mortgaged to Beni Babu for all these years. Last year he bought up everything in repayment of the loan and the interest. But all praise to that woman, Kamini's mother! What the farmer's daughter has done for this poor Brahmin family in their distress is really remarkable. Such instances are indeed rare these days!'

Ramesh sighed and fell silent. He then sent Gopal Sarkar with instructions to make all necessary arrangements.

'Your wishes will be fulfilled, Aunty', he said to himself. 'Even if I have to die here, that's all right by me; but I'll never think of leaving this unfortunate village and going away.'

69

CHAPTER
10

About three months later, one morning, standing on the flight of steps leading up from the water reservoir called Dudhpukur at Tarakeshwar, Ramesh suddenly found himself face to face with a woman. For a moment he was so completely overwhelmed that he continued gazing like an ill-bred person at her uncovered face and it did not occur to him that he should step aside and let her pass. The woman could not have been more than twenty. She was coming up the steps after her bath in the pond. She hurriedly put her water-pot down and placed her two arms across her breast underneath the wet sari, and softly asked, with downcast eyes, 'How's it that you're here?'

Ramesh was greatly surprised, but he was no longer bewildered. He now stepped aside and asked, 'Do you know me?'

'Yes, I do. When did you come to Tarakeshwar?'

'Only this morning. Ladies from my uncle's house were supposed to come here, but they haven't."

'Where're you staying here?'

'Nowhere. I've never been here before. But I'll have to spend the day here somehow, waiting for them. I'll find some accommodation somewhere.'

'Have you got your servant with you?'

'No, I just came alone.'

'Strange!' said the lady, with an amused smile and then, as she looked up, their eyes met again. She at once lowered her eyes, and perhaps hesitated for a moment, and then said, 'Then come along with me.' She lifted her water-pot and got ready to proceed.

Ramesh was in a fix. He said, 'I may as well come along, because had there been anything objectionable in this, you wouldn't have asked me to come with you. Also, it's not that I haven't seen you before, but I can't remember where. Won't you tell me who you are?'

'Then please wait for a while outside the temple. Let me finish my worship. On our way home I'll tell you who I am.' The woman went into the temple. Ramesh continued looking at her receding figure, as if spell-bound.

What an exuberance of youthful beauty, trying to break through the veil of wet clothes! It seemed to Ramesh that her face, her figure, her gait, were all known to him. Yet the long-lost memory seemed to be locked up in some dark chamber and however hard he tried he could not unlock the door to regain it.

After half an hour the lady came out of the temple. Ramesh again saw her face, but the impenetrable wall of unfamiliarity remained as before.

On the way Ramesh asked, 'Haven't you any relatives with you here?'

'No. I've my maid... she's working in the house. I come here every now and then. So I know the place well.'

'But why are you taking me along?'

The lady did not give any reply and kept walking for some time. At last she said, 'Otherwise you'd have had difficulty about meals. I'm Rama.'

Rama served lunch, took her seat in front of him and waited on him until the meal was over. She then gave him a betel leaf, spread a carpet for him to lie down and rest, and went away to another room.

Lying on that bed, with his eyes closed, Ramesh felt as if his twenty-three-year-old life had undergone a complete change within these few hours. Since his childhood he had spent his time away from home, looked after by others. He had never known that a meal could be anything more than just satisfying hunger. So the satisfaction which the meal gave him today was something inconceivable. It filled his heart with a pleasing sensation of sweetness and surprise.

Rama had not been able to arrange any special dishes for him. She served him only ordinary items of food and drink. She was greatly worried lest the simple food should fail to satisfy him, and he might find an excuse to criticize her. O, this fear of others and their fault-finding! How could she hide from herself that hers was the greatest worry and that it was her deep yearning to feed him, entrenched in the innermost recesses of her heart, which had driven her to overcome all hesitation and scruples and invite him to be her guest. Today, not even her own shyness could deter her. She sat in front of him throughout the meal so as to make up for its shortcomings by her tender care and solicitation. When the lunch was over, she heaved a sigh of relief and her own satisfaction was much more than that of Ramesh. Even if none else knew this, it was known to Him who knew everything.

Ramesh was not in the habit of having a siesta in the daytime. Looking out with half-closed eyes through the small window facing him, he found the dark-grey clouds of early rains covering up the midday sky. The thought of the coming or not of his relatives no longer occupied his mind. Suddenly Rama's soft voice floated into his ears. Standing outside the door she was saying, 'Looks like you can't get home today; then why not stay here?'

Ramesh hurriedly sat up and said, 'But I haven't yet seen the owner of the house. How can I stay unless I'm requested by him?'

Rama replied, standing where she was, 'It's the owner who is requesting you. This house is mine.'

Ramesh was surprised. 'Why a house at a place like this?' he asked.

'I like this place very much and come here quite often. There's none else in the house today, but at times it becomes so crowded that it's difficult even to move about.'

'Well, then don't come at such a time.'

Rama smiled silently.

'You have, I believe, great devotion for Lord Taraknath, haven't you?' asked Ramesh again.

'Nothing to speak about. But I have to try, as long as I live', replied Rama.

Ramesh did not ask any more questions. Rama sat down by the side of the doorframe and, changing the subject, asked, 'What do you eat at night?'

Ramesh said with a smile, 'Whatever comes my way. I never think of my meal till the moment I sit down to it. So I've to be satisfied with the good sense of my cook.'

'Why this indifference?'

Ramesh was not sure whether this was concealed mockery or a simple joke. He replied, briefly, 'No, it's simply laziness.'

'But I don't find you lazy while working for others.'

'For a very good reason. If one neglects one's duty to others, one has to stand trial before God. Perhaps it's so even in the case of one's own job, but certainly not to the same extent.'

After a brief silence, Rama said, 'You've enough money, so you can afford to work for others. But what about those who haven't?'

'I don't know about them, Rama. I only know that possession of wealth has no limit; neither is there any end to the interest one can take in other people. All this is known only to Him who is in charge of our present life and the life beyond.'

Rama remained silent for a while and then said, 'But you aren't that old to start thinking of a future life. You're only three years older than I.'

Ramesh smiled. 'That means you're even less old to

start thinking of it. Let it be so! May God give you a long life! But so far as I'm concerned, I can never cease to think for a moment that this may be the last day of my life.'

The deep hurt lying hidden in these words did not perhaps go in vain. Rama kept quiet for some time and then said abruptly, 'I didn't see you doing your midday prayers. You may not have been interested to see what was there inside the temple, but have you even forgotten the ritual sipping of water before starting the meal?'

Ramesh smiled silently and then said; 'No, I haven't; but I don't think there's any harm in forgetting it. But why raise this question?'

'Because you appear to be much concerned with the life hereafter. That's why.'

Ramesh did not reply. Both remained silent for some time. Then Rama began mildly, 'You ought to know that wishing me a long life is as good as cursing me. Among the Hindus no relative ever prays for the long life of a widow.' After a pause she added, 'It's not that I'm craving for an early death, but at the same time I shudder to think of the prospect of a long life for me. Your case is of course different. It'd be impertinent on my part to offer you any advice, but when, later in life, you'll realize that it's sheer childishness to trouble one's head about others, you'll possibly remember what I told you today.'

Ramesh heaved a sigh and kept quiet. After some time he began, as softly as Rama had done. 'But I can tell you that I don't feel like that at all today when I remember what you've just done for me. I'm none to you, Rama; rather I'm more a thorn in your side. Yet what great care you've lavished on me today as a neighbour of yours! I think that those who receive such attention and care from their own dear ones every day, can't help rushing to give succour to all who are in distress. A little while ago, when I was lying all alone in this room, I was thinking to myself how you had completely changed my life within these few hours. Nobody has ever invited me in this manner, nor has anyone ever served food to me with so much care. I've learnt from you, for the first time in my life today, that there can be such joy in eating one's food.'

These words sent a thrill and shiver through Rama. But she steadied herself and said, 'But I'm sure it won't take you long to forget this. And even if you happen to remember it at any time, you'll then treat it as a very trivial affair!'

Ramesh gave no answer.

'However, it's reassuring for me', continued Rama, 'that when you go back home you'll not speak ill of me.'

Ramesh again sighed and said gently, 'No, Rama, I'll not speak ill of you; nor shall I sing praise of you. This day is something very different for me. It's above all abuse and praise.'

Rama did not say anything more and remained silent for some time. She then got up and went away to her own room. There, in the loneliness and privacy of the room, large drops of tears welled up in her eyes and started rolling down her cheeks.

CHAPTER
11

After incessant downpour for two days, the rain stopped for a while towards the afternoon. In the House of Worship Ramesh was sitting beside Gopal Sarkar and going through the accounts of his estate. All on a sudden about twenty peasants came and stood there, all in tears. 'O! Chhoto Babu, please save us this time. Unless you help us, we'll all be ruined and compelled to beg on the roads along with our wives and children!' they cried.

Ramesh was surprised. 'What's the matter?' he asked.

The peasants replied, 'The thirty-acre plot has been flooded. Unless the water is drained out, the paddy crop will be ruined; not a single family in the village will have anything to eat.'

Ramesh was not able to follow them clearly. Gopal Sarkar put some questions to them and then explained the matter to Ramesh.

The thirty-acre plot of land was the only succour of this village. All the peasants possessed some land in that plot. It was bounded on the east by the high government embankment and on the west and the north by the village perched high. The accumulated water could be drained out only through the embankment on the southern side, which belonged to the Ghoshals and Mukharjis. But there was a fish pond in the swamp by the side of the embankment, and the fish fetched an annual income of about two hundred rupees. So the landowner, Beni Babu, had mounted a strong guard to protect the embankment. All through the morning the

76

peasants had grovelled at his feet and had just left the place and come here, crying all the way.

Ramesh did not wait to hear anything more, but rushed out. When he reached Beni's place it was nearing dusk. Beni was reclining on a cushion, enjoying a smoke. Mr. Haldar was sitting by his side. Possibly they were discussing this very matter.

Ramesh did not waste any time on introductory remarks, but went straight to the point.

'It won't do, if we go on guarding the embankment of the swamp any longer. It must be cut immediately.'

Beni handed over the *hookah* to Haldar and, raising his face, asked, 'Which embankment?'

Ramesh was already agitated when he came. He now replied argrily, 'How many embankments are there by the side of the swamp, Dada? If we don't allow the cut, the entire paddy crop of the villagers will rot in the water and be spoiled. Please give orders to drain out the water.'

Beni said, 'But do you know that it'll mean flooding out fish worth two or three hundred rupees? Who'll pay that amount? The peasants or you?'

Controlling his anger, Ramesh said, 'The peasants are too poor to pay. And I don't understand why I should pay.'

'I also don't understand why we should suffer this loss,' retorted Beni. Then looking at Haldar he added, 'Uncle, this is the way brother is going to maintain his estate! Well, Ramesh, those rascals have been here since the morning, crying themselves hoarse. I know everything. Don't you have a watchman at your gate? Doesn't he have tanned leather shoes on his feet? Go home and arrange that... the water'll get drained by itself.' Saying this Beni indulged in his habitual giggling at his own witty remarks, along with Haldar.

Ramesh was unable to put up with it any longer. Yet he restrained himself with a supreme effort and said humbly, 'Dada, please reconsider your decision. If we three families want to avoid our loss of two hundred rupees, the poor people will lose their food for the whole year. Their loss will be at least five to seven thousand rupees.'

Beni turned his hands upside down and said, 'What's that to me? Their loss may be five thousand or fifty thousand... but even if my entire outer courtyard is dug up, it won't yield a two-pice bit. Then why should I suffer a loss of two hundred rupees for the sake of these rascals?'

Ramesh made a last attempt. 'How will they live throughout the year?'

Beni burst into a loud laughter, as if it was a grand joke. In his merriment he rocked back and forth, shook his head this way and that, and spat. At last he steadied himself, and said, 'How'll they live?' You'll see they'll come running to us for loan by mortgaging whatever land they have. Well, my brother, keep your head cool. Our forefathers increased their property in this way, and were thus able to bequeath an estate to us. We have to live ourselves with this as best we can, and then leave something for our children also. How'll the peasants live? By borrowing, that's how. Otherwise why are they called "low-born" people, eh?'

Ramesh felt his face and eyes burning with hatred, shame, anger, and sorrow. Still he spoke in a calm voice, 'As you're determined not to do anything, it's no good arguing with you any longer. I'm going to Rama. If she agrees, then your disapproval alone won't matter.'

Beni became grave. 'All right', he said, 'go and try. You'll find that her views are not different from mine. Mind you, brother, she's not a simple girl.... it's not easy to hoodwink her. Moreover you're just a child compared to her. She didn't even spare your father and made his life miserable. What d'you say, Uncle?'

Ramesh had no curiosity to know what Uncle had to

78

say. Nor was he inclined to give any reply to these most insulting remarks of Beni's. He rushed out without another word.

Rama had just placed the evening lamp at the foot of the sacred basil in the courtyard and made an obeisance. When she raised her head, she was surprised to find Ramesh standing before her. She had the border of her sari wrapped round her neck. It seemed as if she had just raised her face after making a low bow to Ramesh.

In his excitement arising out of anger and anxiety, Ramesh had forgotten the prohibitory order issued by Rama's aunt on the first day of his meeting her and had come straight into the inner courtyard. Finding Rama saying her prayers, Ramesh was waiting silently. This was their first meeting after about a month.

Ramesh said, 'You must've heard everything. I've come to obtain your consent to drain out the water.'

Rama's bewilderment was now over. She pulled the border of her sari over her head and said, 'How's that possible? Besides Dada is not agreeable.'

'I know that, but his dissent alone doesn't matter.'

Rama thought for a few moments and then said, 'It may be desirable to allow the water to drain out, but what arrangements are you going to make to keep the fish from being washed away?'

'Nothing can be done in so much water. We'll have to suffer the loss this year. Otherwise all the villagers will be ruined.'

Rama remained silent.

'Then may I take it that you've given your permission?'

Rama replied in a low voice, 'No, I can't afford to suffer the loss of so much money.'

Ramesh was astounded. He had not expected such a reply from Rama. Rather, he had somehow formed an impression that Rama would never turn down an earnest request from him.

Rama raised her eyes and perhaps at once sensed Ramesh's thoughts. She added, 'Besides, the estate belongs to my younger brother. I'm only his guardian.'

'Oh, no, half the property is yours!'

'That's only in name. My father knew very well that Jatin would get the entire property. So he willed half of it to me.'

Still Ramesh said imploringly, 'It's not a very big sum, Rama. You're the richest people in this part of the country. This loss is negligible for you. I entreat you, Rama, please don't cause starvation to so many people for this small amount. I could never even dream that you could be so cruel.'

Rama replied as mildly as before, 'If you consider me cruel simply because I'm not prepared to suffer any loss, I can't help it. Well, if you're so very kind-hearted, why don't you make up our loss yourself?'

Imagining that her soft tone was nothing but a taunt, Ramesh was filled with rage. He blurted out, 'Well, Rama, a person appears in his true colours where money is involved. Nobody can deceive others in a matter in which his pecuniary interests are concerned.... There his true self is exposed. The same has been the case with you today. But I never imagined that you could be like this. I've always thought you were far, far above all meanness. But I now find that you're not really so. It's a mistake to call you cruel. You're mean, you're low.'

Rama gasped with her eyes wide open in bewilderment. 'What did you say I am?

'I said you were mean and low', cried Ramesh. 'You raised the question of compensation, knowing very well how anxious I was to get this work done. Even Dada couldn't ask for it in so many words. That was too much even for him, a man. You are a woman... yet you didn't have any hesitation in asking for it openly. I can certainly give a much bigger compensation, if necessary. But I tell you that the worst of all sins is to coerce someone, taking advantage of his kindness. You have done that today to extract money from me.'

Rama continued to look on – completely dazed. Not a word fell from her lips.

Ramesh went on in his quiet but firm tone, 'You're no doubt aware of my weakness. But you can't get anything out of it, however hard you may press. At the same time I'm also telling you what I'm going to do now. I shall forcibly make a cut in the embankment. Try to stop it, if you can.'

Seeing that Ramesh was going away, Rama called him back. As soon as he returned and stood near her, Rama said, 'I don't like to say a word in reply to all the insulting things that you've said about me, standing in my own house. But I urge you, please don't try to do this.'

'Why?'

'Because even after so much insult I wouldn't like to quarrel with you.'

Even in the darkness of the evening Ramesh could notice the unusual pallor of her face and the quivering of her lips. But he had neither the time nor the mood to go into an assessment of her psychology. He promptly replied, 'I too don't have the least intention of picking up a quarrel with you. But at the same time your goodwill has lost all its significance for me. In any case, it's no good bandying words with you. I'm going.'

Rama's aunt had been in the room upstairs reserved for the worship of the family deity. So she was not aware of these developments. When she came down, she found Rama going out, accompanied by a maid.

'Where're you going at this hour, through all the mud and slush ?' she asked in surprise.

'I'm just going to Dada's place, Aunt.'

The maid said, 'No, the road's no longer muddy.

Chhoto Babu has got the road re-done in such a way that you can now pick up even a speck of vermilion from it. May God give him long life!... the poor wretches are now safe from snakebite.'

It was 11 o'clock at night. The hushed voices of a number of people could be heard from Beni's House of Worship. The clouds in the sky had somewhat cleared. It was the thirteenth night of the new moon. A frosty moonlight fell on the porch. There, leaning against a pillar, was seated a fierce-looking elderly Mussalman, with his eyes shut. His face was spattered with patches of clotted fresh blood. The clothes he wore were red with blood. But he was quiet.

Beni was beseeching him in a low voice, 'Listen to me, Akbar. Let's go to the police station. If I can't put him in jail for at least seven years, I shall no longer claim to be a scion of the Ghoshal family.' Looking back at Rama, Beni added, 'Why don't you request Akbar, Rama? Why are you silent?' But Rama remained mute, rooted to the ground like a wooden statue.

Akbar Ali now opened his eyes, sat straight and said, 'Well done! Yes – Chhoto Babu has really fed on his mother's milk! How skilfully he wielded the bamboo stave!'

Agitated and angry, Beni cried, 'Well, that's exactly what I'm asking you to say, Akbar. Tell me, whose blow wounded you... that fellow's or his up-country servant's?'

An amused smile played on Akbar's lips. He said, 'That short-statured up-country man? What does that fellow know of bamboo staves, Babu? What d'you say, Gahar? Your very first blow felled him, didn't it?'

Akbar's two sons were sitting at a short distance, huddled together. They were also wounded. Gahar nodded his head in the affirmative, but gave no reply. Akbar continued, 'That fellow would've fallen dead if he had received a blow from me. As soon as he was hit by Gahar's stave, he fell down with a cry.

Rama got up and came nearer. Akbar was one of her tenants from Pirpur. In the past he had helped the Mukharjis in acquiring new property, forcibly, with the help of his stave. So this evening, maddened with rage and offended pride, Rama had sent for him and asked him to guard the embankment. She wanted to see what Ramesh could do with the help of his up-country servant alone. But she had not the faintest idea that Ramesh was himself such a great wielder of the stave. It was something beyond her imagination.

Akbar looked up at Rama and said, 'Chhoto Babu then picked up that man's stave in his own hands and blocked our way, Young Mistress. We three couldn't force him to move even an inch. In the darkness his eyes flashed and glowed like a tiger's. He told me, "Akbar, you're an old man.... go away. Unless the embankment is cut, all the villagers will die of starvation. So it'll have to be cut in any case. You have your own cultivable land in your village, haven't you? Just think for a moment how you'd feel if your own crop was ruined." I saluted him and said, "Chhoto Babu, in the name of Allah, allow me to advance and catch hold of these rogues, who have covered their faces and are briskly chopping up the embankment with their spades, shielded safely behind you. Let me crack their skulls!"'

Beni could not control his anger any longer and shouted in the midst of Akbar's talk, 'You ungrateful wretches! You salute him and then come and show your cleverness here!'

Akbar and his two sons immediately raised their hands. Akbar shouted harshly, 'Take care, Babu! Don't call us ungrateful! We're Mussalmans... we can tolerate everything, but not that!'

He wiped the blood from his forehead and said to Rama, 'He's calling us ungrateful, Didi! You're sitting in

83

your own room and calling us ungrateful, Babu! If you had seen with your own eyes, you'd have known what Chhoto Babu is!'

'What Chhoto Babu is!' mimicked Beni with a grimace. 'Why don't you go and say just that at the police station! You've simply to say that you were guarding the embankment and Chhoto Babu came and attacked and assaulted you!'

Akbar bit his tongue and said, 'God forbid! Shame! you ask me to call the day night, Babu!'

Beni said, 'Well, you may say something else if you like. But show your wounds to the police tonight. Tomorrow I'll get a warrant of arrest issued against him and clap him in jail. Rama, why don't you explain everything clearly to him? We'll never get such an opportunity again in future.'

Rama said nothing, but looked at Akbar's face once. Akbar shook his head and said, 'No, Young Mistress, we can't do that.'

Beni thundered, 'Why can't you?'

This time Akbar also shouted, 'What d'you say, Babu! Don't I have any shame? Am I not regarded by the people of the five adjacent villages as their chief? If you order me, Didi, I'm prepared to go to jail as an accused. But how can I be so shameless as to become a complainant?'

Rama spoke just for once, in a low voice, 'Can't you do this, Akbar?'

Akbar shook his head violently and said, 'No, dear Didi, I can do everything, but I can't go to the police station and show my wounds there. Get up, Gahar, let's go home. We can't go and lodge a complaint.' Akbar stood up and got ready to leave.

Beni looked on helplessly, angry and desperate. It seemed as if his two eyes were hurling shafts of fire to burn Akbar to ashes. In his heart of hearts, Beni called Akbar all sorts of ugly names. He failed to understand why Rama was keeping silent in this way. He seethed with rage and felt as if a smouldering fire of husks was slowly burning him.

When at last Akbar Ali left with his two sons, disregarding Beni's entreaties, reproaches and indignation, a long and deep sigh came out of Rama's breast and for an unknown reason her eyes filled with tears. In spite of all the insult and defeat of that evening, she felt greatly relieved as if a heavy load of stone had been lifted from her heart. The reason for this was not quite clear to her. On returning home, she could not have a wink of sleep that night. The picture of Ramesh eating lunch in her presence at Tarakeshwar appeared again and again before her mind's eye. As she recollected how so much tenderness and strength could reside harmoniously side by side in his handsome and graceful body, tears welled up in her eyes and fell in large drops down her cheeks.

CHAPTER
12

Ramesh had once fallen in love with Rama in his child-hood. Undoubtedly it was then but a child's fancy. Yet when Ramesh met Rama at Tarakeshwar, he realized for the first time how deep and profound that love was. He realized it once more on that fateful evening when he quarrelled with Rama and came away from her house snapping all ties with her. Since that tragic night every-thing connected with Rama appeared to him as dreary and barren as a desert. But he had not the faintest idea that this would make his life – all his work, his food and drink, his sleep, his study and even his thoughts – insipid and bitter. To add to his misery, there was the quarrel with Beni and the general atmosphere of hostil-ity in the village. When life had become almost intoler-able for him, the following incident again gave him back his enthusiasm for work.

The village of Pirpur on the other side of the canal formed a part of the estate of the Ghoshals and Mukharjis. The majority of the population there were Muslims. One day they came in a body to meet Ramesh. They complained that although they were their tenants, their sons were not admitted into the village school on the ground that they were Muslims. They had failed in their attempt several times; the teachers could not be persuaded to admit their boys. Ramesh was surprised as well as angry. 'I've never heard of such an injustice before', he said. 'Bring all your boys today. I'll person-ally take them to the school and get them admitted.''

They informed Ramesh that unlike the Hindu tenants, they paid their rent in cash. Hence they were not as much afraid of the landowner as the Hindu tenants were. But in any case a quarrel would be of no use. It would necessarily cause unpleasantness, but would not produce the desired results. So they preferred to open a small school of their own at Pirpur and solicited Chhoto Babu's help for this purpose. Ramesh was already tired of quarrels and disputes. So he agreed that it was better not to get into further quarrels, and accepted their suggestion. Since then he devoted himself completely to the opening of a new school at Pirpur.

Coming in contact with the Muslims of Pirpur, Ramesh not only regained his peace of mind, but also found that he was recovering all the energy he had lost during the preceding year. Ramesh noticed that the Muslims did not quarrel among themselves on petty issues as their Hindu neighbours of Kuanpur did, and even when they quarrelled, they did not run to the district headquarters to file lawsuits against their opponents. Rather they accepted ungrudgingly the decisions given by the village elders, whether it satisfied them immediately or not. Moreover, they came forward to help their neighbours most wholeheartedly at the time of their difficulty. Ramesh had not seen any Hindu villager, whether of high birth or low, render such assistance to his Hindu neighbour in his distress.

Ramesh had never any faith in the caste system. Now, when he compared the condition prevailing in the two neighbouring villages, his distaste for the caste system increased a hundredfold. He was convinced that the religious and social inequality among the Hindus was responsible for the canker of hatred and malice among them. On the other hand, all Muslims were equal so far as religion was concerned. Therefore, there was a strong bond of unity among them. The Hindus had no such bond of unity, nor was it possible. And as it was impossible to remove the caste restrictions – it was even impossible to raise such a question in a village – it was sheer waste of energy trying to bring down the number of quarrels and disputes and establish amity and fraternity among them. He now began to regret that he had taken so much trouble for improving the condition in his village during these years. He had now no doubt in his mind that these people would go on quarrelling among themselves, as they had always done in the past. There could never be any real improvement in this matter. But he felt he should get his opinion confirmed.

For various reasons Ramesh had not been able to meet Aunty for quite some time. After that fight on the embankment he had purposely avoided going that way. Aunty herself was unaware of the amount of regard that Ramesh had for her wisdom and experience. This morning, immediately after he got up, Ramesh went straight to Aunty's house and stood outside her door. He was surprised to find that Aunty had already finished her bath at this early hour of the morning. She was sitting on the floor and in the dim light reading a book. Aunty was also surprised to see Ramesh so early in the morning. She shut the book, greeted him affectionately and offered him a seat by her side. Then she looked at him and asked, 'How's it that you've come so early in the morning?'

'I couldn't come and see you for a long time. I'm opening a school at Pirpur.'

'I've heard about it. But why don't you take classes in our village school any longer?'

'I've come to tell you just that. I find that it's futile trying to do any good to these people here. They are envious of others; they are too full of pride and arrogance. However hard one may work for them, it's never appreciated, only the number of one's enemies increases. I'd rather work for those who'd really benefit from my labours.'

'There's nothing new in what you say, Ramesh. It's usual to find that the number of one's enemies increases when one takes upon oneself the task of doing good to others. There are some who are afraid of this and back out. It won't do for you too to join the rank of deserters. God has placed this heavy burden on your shoulders and you've to carry it throughout your life....Now, Ramesh, is it a fact that you accept drinking water from the hands of the Muslims?'

Ramesh laughed. 'Strange that the rumour should've already reached your ears! I haven't yet done so, but I don't see any harm in doing that. I don't believe in your caste prejudices and restrictions, Aunty.'

Aunty was surprised. 'What d'you mean?' she asked. 'The caste system is very much there. So how can you say that you don't believe in it?'

Ramesh said, 'It's exactly this point which I wanted to discuss with you today, Aunty. I know the caste system exists, but I don't believe that it is a good thing.'

'Why not?'

Ramesh suddenly became agitated and cried, 'Why? Need I tell you that too? Don't you know that all the ill-will, all the quarrels have arisen out of caste restrictions? It seems to me very natural that those who have been branded by the society as "low-caste" should be envious of the high-caste people, and revolt against this custom and try to free themselves from its fetters. Hindus don't know how to acquire, they don't even want to do so – they simply know how to squander! There's a natural law which requires that one should not only protect oneself and one's society and preserve it intact, but one should also try to augment it. We Hindus don't observe that law. That's why our number dwindles every day. There's a law for the periodical enumeration of the population of this country. Had you read the census reports, you'd have been frightened, Aunty. You'd then have known what's the result of insulting and branding a section of the Hindu population as "low-caste". You'd then come to know how the number of Hindus is dwindling every year and the number of Muslims is increasing. Yet the Hindus don't come to their senses!'

Bishweshwari smiled. 'Well, I haven't come to my senses even after hearing all that you've said! If the enumerators could tell me that so many Hindus have renounced their ancestral faith and embraced Islam simply because they were treated as "low-caste", then possibly I'd have been worried. I agree that the number of Hindus is decreasing every year, but the reason for that is different – of course the society is responsible even for that – but it's not as a result of change of their religious faith by the low-caste Hindus. No Hindu has ever renounced his faith simply because he was called "low-caste".'

Ramesh was still sceptical. 'But that's what the scholars surmise, Aunty', he said.

'Well, there can be no argument against a surmise. If one could give me definite information that so-and-so "low-caste" Hindu of such-and-such village has renounced Hinduism and become a Muslim just because he was treated as "low-caste", then possibly I'd have accepted the views of your pundits. But I'm sure nobody'll be able to give me that information.'

Ramesh continued to argue. 'But it seems to me that it's only natural that the low-caste people should be envious of the high-caste people.'

The agitated manner in which he argued caused Bishweshwari amusement. 'It's not at all true, my boy, not at all true! Villages aren't like towns. In a village nobody bothers his head about the question of low-caste and high-caste. Just as a younger brother has no grievance against his elder brother simply because he was born one or two years later, and doesn't envy his elder brother on that account, in the same way a Kayastha is not at all sorry that he wasn't born a Brahmin, and a fisherman doesn't try to be the equal of a Kayastha. Just as a younger brother isn't ashamed of bowing down before his elder brother, a Kayastha doesn't feel embarrassed to make obeisance before a Brahmin. No, Ramesh, the caste system isn't responsible for the mutual hatred and ill-will among the Hindus – at least it's not so in the villages, which are the backbone of the Bengali society.'

Ramesh was surprised and asked, 'Then why does this happen, Aunty? The Muslims of Pirpur don't quarrel among themselves in this way. There one doesn't harass another in his hour of distress as the Hindus do. I'm sure you know that nobody was willing to touch the corpse of Dwarik Thakur because the prescribed expiatory rites couldn't be performed in time for want of money.'

'Yes, I know all that. But the caste system isn't the reason for such superstitious belief. The reason is this: the Muslims have a living religion, but the Hindus haven't. What they call "true religion" has, in fact, completely disappeared from the villages; what is left are the superstitious customs and practices which give rise to needless strifes and bickerings.'

Ramesh sighed in despair. 'Is there no remedy then, Aunty?'

'Certainly there is, my son. The remedy lies in enlightenment, in true knowledge. It lies in the path you've chosen. That's why I tell you again and again not to leave your birthplace and go away.'

Ramesh was about to say something in reply, but Bishweshwari interrupted him and said, 'You may say that there's great ignorance among the Muslims too. But their living religion has made up for all such deficiency. Now listen, Ramesh. If you make enquiries at Pirpur, you'll come to know that one rich man named Jafar has been excommunicated by his community because he didn't support his widowed stepmother. But when our Govinda Ganguly beat the widow of his elder brother within an inch of her life with his own hands the other day, the community took no action to punish him. Rather he continued to be one of its leaders as before. Among the Hindus such offence is only a question of one's own personal virtue or vice. God may punish one for that if He likes, but the village community takes no notice of it.'

This was a new theory which Ramesh had not heard before. While it surprised him on the one hand, he was still hesitant to accept it as truth, on the other. Bishweshwari could sense Ramesh's hesitation and said, 'Never mistake the means as the end, my son. The reason why you can't shake off your doubts from your mind – the issue of the tussle between the low-caste and the high-caste – is only a symptom of progress, not its cause. If you think that must come first, if you devote yourself to that only, all your efforts will be spoilt. If you wish to verify the truth of what I am saying, go round a few villages near a town and compare the condition prevailing there with that of Kuanpur. You'll yourself realize I'm right.'

Ramesh had close knowledge of one or two villages near Calcutta. He tried to take a mental note of the overall picture in those villages. All on a sudden it seemed to him that the dark screen, which had been suspended before his eyes all the time, restricting his vision, had lifted, and truth dawned on him. Full of surprise and deep reverence for Bishweshwari, Ramesh sat gazing at her face.

Paying no heed to it, Bishweshwari continued, 'That's why I urge you again and again not to leave your birthplace, Ramesh. If men like you, who were brought up and educated away from the villages, would've come back to the villages and not cut off all connection with them, they wouldn't have been reduced to this miserable condition. Then the village community wouldn't have honoured men like Govinda Ganguly and driven away men like you.'

Remembering Rama's attitude towards him, Ramesh said in an injured tone, 'Nor would I mind being driven away now, Aunty.'

Bishweshwari noticed this tone but could not understand the reason behind this. 'No Ramesh, that won't do!' she said. 'Once you've come here, you mustn't leave your work unfinished. Your birthplace won't forgive you ever if you do that.'

'But why, Aunty? The birthplace isn't mine alone.'

Aunty seemed inspired. 'Yes, it's only yours, my son. She's your mother only. Don't you see that she never claimed any sacrifice from anyone else before? That's why none heard her cries... but you did so as soon as you arrived.'

Ramesh did not argue any longer. He kept quiet for some time, then silently made a deep obeisance to Bishweshwari and taking the dust from her feet went out.

As he walked home, his heart was full of reverence, compassion, and devotion to duty.

When Ramesh returned home, the sun was just up in the eastern sky. Standing in front of the open window of his room, he looked out at the sky, completely spellbound.

Suddenly the spell was broken by a child's call. Startled, Ramesh turned and saw that Rama's younger brother Jatin was calling him 'Dada' from outside the door, blushing in shyness. Ramesh went to him, took him by the hands and leading him inside, asked, 'Who were you calling, Jatin?'

'You.'

'Me? Who taught you to call me Dada?'

'Didi.'

'Didi? Has she sent any message to me?'

Jatin shook his head. 'Didi said, "Take me with you to your Ramesh-da's house... ." She's standing there!' He turned and looked at the door.

Surprised, Ramesh hurriedly came over and found Rama standing there behind a pillar. He came round and said humbly, 'It's indeed my good fortune that you've come to my house! But why did you take the trouble of coming yourself instead of sending for me? Anyway, do come in.'

Rama hesitated a little and then catching hold of Jatin's hand followed Ramesh. When she came to the doorway she sat down by the door frame, and said, 'I've come to your house today to beg for some thing... promise me you'll give it!' She fixed her gaze on Ramesh's face.

There was something in that gaze which filled Ramesh's heart to the brim and sent a thrill through him. All the seven strings of his heart reverberated to a maddening crescendo and then broke.

It seemed to Ramesh as if all his resolves, hopes, and aspirations, which had been dancing joyfully in his mind a moment before, were extinguished and plunged into total darkness. Yet he asked, 'What's it you want?'

The unnatural dryness of his tone did not escape Rama's notice. She continued looking at him and said, 'You must first promise.'

Ramesh remained silent for some time and then shook his head and said, 'I can't do that, Rama. You yourself have broken my strength to give you whatever you wanted, without any question.'

Rama was surprised. 'I?....'

'Nobody else had the power to do so, Rama. I'll confess to you today. Believe me if you like; if not, don't. But had it not become already dead and past, perhaps I would never have been able to tell you this.' After a brief silence, he resumed. 'Today it doesn't affect either of us in the least. So I can very well tell you that till the other day there was nothing of my own which I wouldn't have given you just for the asking. But do you know why?'

Rama shook her head to show that she did not know. But her heart began to quiver in apprehension of something embarrassing about to follow.

Ramesh said, 'Don't be angry or feel embarrassed at what I'm going to tell you. Just think for a moment that you're listening to a fairy tale of the past.'

Rama wanted to stop Ramesh with all her strength, but her head hung and she could not raise it at all.

Ramesh went on in his gentle, calm and impersonal voice. 'I loved you, Rama! It seems to me today that no man has ever loved a woman more deeply and profoundly. In my childhood, my mother used to tell me that we two would be married. On the day when all my hopes were shattered, I burst into tears. I still remember it.'

Ramesh's words entered Rama's ears like molten lead and burnt them. It seemed to her that an intolerably intense and severe pain caused by a strange and unknown sensation had begun to pierce her heart through and through, cutting it up into small bits. Not knowing how to stop Ramesh, and feeling utterly helpless, she remained rooted to the ground like a statue, listening to the bittersweet words of Ramesh in spite of herself.

Ramesh continued, 'You may think it's wrong on my part to tell you all this. I too had such doubts in my mind before. So I didn't tell you anything when I met you at Tarakeshwar and with your loving care you completely changed the course of my life in one day. I still remained silent, but, believe me, it wasn't easy for me to do that.'

Rama was not able to endure any longer. 'Then why are you insulting me today taking advantage of my presence in your house?' she cried.

'Insult? Nothing of the sort', said Ramesh. 'There's no question of insult or respect in it. You were never the

Rama of my story and I'm no longer the same Ramesh either. However, please hear me out. I don't know why, but that day I wholeheartedly believed that whatever you might do or say, you'd never entertain the thought of any harm to me. Perhaps I thought that you hadn't yet been able to forget the love which you once had for me in your childhood. So I thought that I'd go on doing my life's work sitting under your shadow, without even telling you anything about it. Then when I heard, on that fateful night, from Akbar's own lips that you had ordered him – but what's that noise outside?'

'Babu!...'

Ramesh was drawn by Gopal Sarkar's agitated cry and rushed out.

'Babu, the police have arrested Bhajua,' spluttered Gopal excitedly.

'Why?'

Gopal was so frightened that his lips were trembling. He said with an effort, 'They say Bhajua was involved in the armed robbery which took place at Radhanagar the night before the last.'

Ramesh turned back towards his room and said, 'Go away at once, Rama; go through the back-door. The police'll certainly search the whole house.'

Rama's face turned deathly pale. She got up and said, 'You are in no danger, are you?'

'I can't say', replied Ramesh. 'I don't know where the matter lies?'

Rama's lips began to tremble. She remembered her own complaint to the police the other day. Suddenly she burst into tears and said, 'I won't go.'

Ramesh was much too surprised to say anything for a moment. Then he said, 'For shame, Rama! You mustn't be found here. Go away immediately.' Without waiting for a word from Rama he took hold of Jatin and dragged the brother and the sister up to the back-door, pushed them out through it and closed it.

CHAPTER
13

For the last two months Bhajua has been in the police lock-up as an undertrial prisoner along with the other accused in the armed robbery case. Although nothing incriminating was found during the search of Ramesh's house that day, and although Bhairab Acharjya gave evidence to the effect that Bhajua had accompanied him to the house of his daughter's prospective bridegroom on the night in question, Bhajua was not released on bail.

One morning Beni came to see Rama. 'Now you see, Rama,' he said, 'you've to consider all possible moves and take action. Only then can you get your enemy into your clutches. If you hadn't reported to the police that Bhajua had trespassed upon your premises, bamboo stave in hand, to claim his master's share of the catch under his orders, it wouldn't have been so easy to lay hands on him. If at the same time you had added something more to your story and implicated Ramesh also... but you didn't listen to my suggestion at the time!'

Rama became so pale that even Beni noticed it. 'No, no,' he said, 'don't worry. You won't have to give evidence in this case. But if it becomes absolutely necessary, what then ? You must be prepared for all such things if you wish to protect your estate.'

Rama remained silent.

Beni continued, 'But we won't get Ramesh in our clutches so easily. He has also made a very clever move. The new school which he has opened at Pirpur will be a source of constant trouble for us. Even in normal times the Muslim tenants don't care much for us. If they become educated, they'll simply defy us. Then there won't be much point in our having our estates.'

Rama had always followed Beni's advice in all matters concerning her estate. There was never any difference of opinion between them. For the first time today, Rama raised an argument. 'But certainly Ramesh-da would be equally affected,' she said.

Beni had his own misgivings in this matter. He had given deliberate consideration to this question and come to some conclusion. He now explained it to Rama. 'You see, Rama, Ramesh doesn't think of his self-interest at all..... He's just interested in humiliating us. Don't you see how he has been squandering money since he came here? There's a regular craze for "Chhoto Babu" among the low-born people as if he is the only person who matters and the two of us are nobodies. But this won't last long, I can assure you. You've very cleverly placed him under the police surveillance. That alone will bring about his ruin in the end. Don't you worry.'

Beni had anticipated that this piece of news would make Rama enthusiastic and excited, but he was surprised to notice that nothing like that happened. On the contrary she looked extremely pale when she asked, 'Does Ramesh-da know that I reported against Bhajua?'

'I'm not sure', replied Beni. 'But of course he'll come to know about it. All this will come to light during the hearing of Bhajua's case.'

Rama did not say anything more. She was trying to recover from the rude shock which Beni's words had given her. It occurred to her again and again that now Ramesh would come to know that it was she alone who was playing the leading role in causing trouble to him. After some time she looked up and asked, 'So his name is heard on everybody's lips these days, is it?'

'Not only in this village,' said Beni. 'I'm told that fol-lowing his example, the people of five or six neighbour-ing villages are taking steps to open schools and to construct roads. Nowadays all the low-born people have started saying that the British could become prosperous only because each village in England has one or two schools. Ramesh has announced that wherever a new school is opened, he'd donate two hundred rupees, and that he'd spend all the money which he has inherited from his grandfather in this way. The Muslims are in fact treating him as if he were something of a prophet!'

A thought arose in Rama's mind which illuminated her heart like a flash of lightning – if only her own name were also associated with Ramesh's ! – but it was for a moment only, and then complete darkness enveloped her heart.

Beni continued, 'But I'm not going to spare him so easily either. Let no one think even in his dreams that we landowners will silently watch with our eyes open and mouth shut, while he goes on inciting our tenants until they get out of hand. I'll deal with that fellow Bhairab Acharjya who had the cheek to give evidence in favour of Bhajua. I'll see how he is able to celebrate his daughter's marriage. I've a plan... let's see what Gov-inda Uncle says about it ! Besides, every now and then there's an armed robbery here and there. If once we can put the servant into prison, it won't be difficult for us to put the master also there. You'll remember, Rama, how you told me on the very first day of Ramesh's arrival at Kuanpur that this man would prove himself to be as formidable an enemy as his father! At that time I didn't really believe that your prophecy would turn out to be so true !'

Rama remained silent. Normally a woman should feel proud that her prophecy had come true and her face beam with joy. But nothing like that happened in this case. On the other hand, Rama's face grew dark and gloomy. Beni was incapable of comprehending her misery. But the change in Rama's expression was so perceptible that it would not escape anybody's notice – it did not escape Beni's either. It perplexed him. He went to the kitchen and after a few words with Rama's aunt, turned to leave. Rama beckoned him back. As he came nearer, Rama asked mildly, 'Won't it be disgraceful for us if Ramesh-da is sent to jail?'

'Why?' asked Beni, greatly surprised.

'After all he's our relation. If we don't save him, won't the people speak ill of us?'

'As he has sown, so shall he reap. What's that to us !' replied Beni.

Rama said as mildly as before, 'But Ramesh-da didn't really commit any burglary or robbery. Rather he's spending his own money, every pie of it, for doing good to others. If we manage to send him to jail, it won't remain a secret. Thereafter how would we show our face to the villagers ?'

This set Beni cackling for quite some time. Then he said, 'What's happened to you, sister ?'

Rama compared this man's face with that of Ramesh, which she mentally conjured up. She felt so miserable that her head hung down in shame. She added, 'Well, even if the people don't say anything to our face out of fear, they'll certainly speak ill of us behind our back. You might say that behind the king's back people call even his mother a witch. But won't God come to know everything ? Will He spare us if we harass an innocent man for no fault of his ?'

'Oh my goodness!' said Beni in mock exasperation. 'Do you think that fellow has any respect for gods and goddesses ? The temple of Goddess Shitala is crumbling for want of repairs. But when I sent a man to request him to meet the expenses for the repairs, he drove him away saying, "Go tell those who've sent you that I've no money for such useless expenditure". Mind you, this is

100

useless expenditure for him, but spending money for opening a school for the Mussalmans is necessary expenditure, if you please ! Besides, he's a Brahmin's son, but he doesn't even say his daily prayers. They say he even drinks water offered by the Muslims. A little English education seems to have turned his head completely. He has renounced all religious practices and has lost his caste. But he can't escape punishment for his sins. They're just piling up and he'll have to pay heavily one day. Everybody will then be convinced of this man's sinfulness.'

Rama did not continue the argument and remained silent. But Beni's words produced their desired effect. Ramesh's non-observance of the customary religious practices and his unorthodox views and lack of respect for gods and goddesses created an unfavourable impression on her mind. Beni went his way, muttering to himself. Rama remained standing quietly at that place for a long time, and then went to her room and slumped heavily on the floor. That was the day of the ritual fast. She felt relieved that she would not have the bother of a meal that day.

CHAPTER
14

The rains were over. The atmosphere in rural Bengal –
its sky, air, and light – was full of an anticipation of joy
for the oncoming Durga Puja and dread for malarial
fever. Ramesh too had an attack of fever. The year
before he had been able to escape the attack of this
demoness, but he could not succeed this year. After
suffering for three days, he got up in the morning and
gulped down a large dose of quinine. Then looking out
through the open window at the yellow rays of the sun,
he began to wonder whether it would be possible to
make the villagers conscious of the danger from the
useless ditches and undergrowth in the village. Three
days' suffering had convinced him that something must
be done. If he took no action and allowed the villagers to
suffer from malaria month after month every year, God
would not forgive him. He had discussed this matter
with the villagers a few days ago. He found that they
were not completely ignorant of the danger from the
ditches and undergrowth. But nobody was prepared to
do any labour of love and take the trouble of filling up
other people's ditches and cutting other people's
brushes. Those who had their own ditches and brushes,
argued that these were there from the time of their
ancestors and they were not responsible for them. They
had no objection if others, who were interested, offered
to fill up those ditches and cut down the undergrowth at
their own cost, but they were unable to spend any
money or energy for it themselves. Ramesh's enquiries
revealed that in many cases, out of two adjacent villages

one was almost free from malaria while the other was ravaged by it. He thought that once he was a little better, he would visit one of those villages which was free from malaria, and see the condition obtaining there with his own eyes, and decide what to do. He was sure that the malaria-free villages had some advantage of natural drainage, and if this could be demonstrably pointed out to the people, they would be convinced; at least his Muslim tenants of Pirpur, who were devoted to him, would co-operate with him. He felt happy that he had at last got an opportunity to put to good use his training as an engineer.

'Chhoto Babu !'

Suddenly attracted by someone's howling, Ramesh turned round and found that Bhairab Acharjya had thrown himself down on the floor and was sobbing bitterly like a woman. One of his daughters, about seven or eight years old, who had come with him, joined her father and filled the room with her wailing. All who were in the house at the time came running and crowded near the door. Ramesh was bewildered. He could not make out what the matter was – whether anyone had died in Bhairab's house or some other calamity had befallen him. He was at a loss to decide who he should question to find out the facts and how he should stop this man's howling. Gopal Sarkar left his own work and rushed there. As he caught hold of Bhairab's hands and pulled him, Bhairab sat up on the floor, flung his hands round Gopal's neck and set up a piteous wail. Remembering that Bhairab was in the habit of bursting into tears at the slightest provocation, like a woman, Ramesh was gradually losing patience. At last Gopal succeeded in consoling and pacifying Bhairab. The latter wiped his tears and became a bit calm. He then narrated the reason for his loud lamentations. Ramesh was astounded by his story. He could not imagine that such tyranny could have ever been perpetrated anywhere.

103

It was like this : After Bhajua had been released on the strength of Bhairab's evidence, Ramesh sent his servant away to his home in order to keep him away from the over-solicitous eyes of the police. Though the accused escaped, the witness was trapped. Having somehow scented danger in the air, Bhairab had gone to the district headquarters the previous day. There he came to know that five or six days ago, one Sanat Mukharji of Radhanagar, Beni Ghoshal's uncle by marriage, had got a decree from the court against Bhairab for a sum of eleven hundred twenty-six rupees and seven annas, and in execution of the decree had seized Bhairab's house on the strength of a distraint warrant issued by the court. It was not an *ex parte* decree. Summons were duly issued. Someone had received it in the name of Bhairab by putting his signature and on the appointed day had presented himself before the court as Bhairab and admitted the plaintiff's claim. The whole affair was a fabrication – the loan was false, the plaintiff false, the defendant false. By virtue of this wholesale and all-embracing falsehood, a rich man had managed to grab all that a poor man possessed and reduced him to utter poverty. But it was not easy to get redress from the court against this tyranny. If Bhairab wanted to challenge the proceedings of the court, he was required under the law first to deposit the entire amount of the decreed money in the court. Otherwise nobody would pay any heed to him, however hard he might protest against the injustice. But where could poor Bhairab get so much money that he would deposit it in the court and then pray for redress against the great injustice done to him ? Therefore, in spite of the fact that there were laws enacted by the government and there were courts, judges, and magistrates, the poor man would have to suffer silently. Nobody had any doubt that this was all Beni's and Govinda Ganguly's machination, but however great might be Bhairab's sufferings, nobody would raise his little finger against this tyranny. The villagers would secretly discuss the matter among themselves, but nobody would protest openly against this high-handedness. They would declare that they were quite unconcerned in this matter and that they did not like poking their nose into other people's affairs.

However, it was now clear to Ramesh how these unscrupulous persons became bold enough to harass the poor villagers unhesitatingly, and how they made use of the laws of the land like a butcher's knife, to further their own interests. While their money and shrewdness afforded them protection from the hands of the police and the law courts, the moribund village community did not punish them for their misdeeds. That is how these people managed to escape scot-free for all the offences committed by them and managed to thrive in utter disregard of the village community.

Ramesh remembered again and again what Aunty had told him sometime ago. She had said with a pathetic smile on her lips, 'Ramesh, forget all your notions and disputes about the mischief done by the caste-system. Only light the lamps everywhere; give them enlightenment... give them knowledge ! Ignorance has made the villagers blind. Give them the light to see with their own eyes ! Then they'll be able to know what's black and what's white.' She had also said, 'Once you've come here, don't ever go away ! Your place of birth has come to this miserable condition simply because you educated people don't pay any attention to it.' Quite true ! If he had gone away, no steps would have been taken to improve its condition.

Ramesh sighed despairingly and said to himself, 'Alas! this is the thing of which we are so proud – our pure, peaceful and just village community. Perhaps at one time it was a living reality and then it had the power to punish the guilty and to protect those who obeyed it and to help them in their life's journey. But today it was dead. Yet the blind villagers didn't leave its corpse alone, but clung to it out of a wrong attachment for it, and carried the heavy and putrid carcass on their heads, day after day. This had made them so tired, feeble and weak, that they were blind to their own deplorable condition. In their mistaken belief in that dead thing, which gave no protection to the oppressed but only caused them further sufferings, the villagers were guilty of a sin which was dragging them along down the path of degradation and perdition.'

Ramesh sat quietly for a little while and then suddenly got up with a start. He immediately wrote out a cheque for the entire amount of the decree, handed it over to Gopal Sarkar and said, 'Deposit this amount in the court after making full enquiries. Make all necessary arrangements for reconsideration of the case. Let not those rascals have the courage to perpetrate such outrageous tyranny again in future !'

Both Gopal Sarkar, with the cheque in his hand, and Bhairab looked on for some time with a dazed look. Ramesh repeated what he had already said. When it became quite clear that he was not joking but was in earnest, Bhairab came and fell at his feet. He then clasped Ramesh's feet frantically and began to howl like a madman and blessed him over and over again and created such a scene that Ramesh could extricate himself from Bhairab's grip only with difficulty. It would have been almost impossible for anyone less sturdy than Ramesh to do so.

Within a short time everyone in the village heard about this affair. They were all convinced that Beni and Govinda would not be able to escape punishment so easily this time. They talked among themselves that Chhoto Babu had risked such a large sum of money only to get his old enemies in his clutches. What none of them imagined was that God had shifted this heavy burden from the weak shoulders of Bhairab and placed it on the broad shoulders of one who would be able to bear it without difficulty.

About a month passed after this incident. Ramesh,

who had declared a silent war against malaria, remained busy during this one month in enthusiastically surveying different areas with the help of his instruments. He had totally forgotten that Bhairab's case was due to come up for hearing the next day. In the evening flute-strains suddenly reminded him of the fact. On making enquiries from his servants, Ramesh came to know that the ceremony of feeding the first rice to Bhairab's grandson was taking place that day. Ramesh was surprised that he knew nothing about it. He was told that Bhairab had made fairly good arrangements and had invited everyone in the village to the feast. However, nobody in his house could tell him whether anyone had come to invite him or not. To add to his surprise, Ramesh now remembered that although such a serious case hung over his head, Bhairab had not met him even once during the past twenty or twenty-five days. What could the matter be? But it did not occur to him even once that of all persons, he might have been excluded by Bhairab from the list of invitees. Ramesh felt ashamed that he could even think of such a possibility. Throwing a scarf round his shoulders, he set out directly for Bhairab's house.

When he arrived there, Ramesh saw that some stray dogs were quarrelling near the fence over the remnants of food in piles of banana leaves; the musicians were seated around a fire at a little distance, warming their musical instruments and enjoying a smoke. He entered the courtyard and found that an old and tattered canopy had been pitched there and five or six very old kerosene lamps, which were the only ones available in the whole village and had been borrowed from the Mukharjis and the Ghoshals, were burning there. They were giving scanty light, but the profuse smoke emitted by them had filled the entire place with an offensive smell. The feast was already over and there were not many people there. The village elders were getting ready to go. Dharmadas was pressing Harihar Ray to stay a bit longer. Govinda

Ganguly, who was sitting apart, was engaged in a private talk with a farmer's son. All on a sudden Ramesh appeared at the centre of the courtyard like a bad dream. All present turned pale at his sight. The fact that one or two members of the enemy's camp had attended the function in this house so eagerly did not please Ramesh either. Nobody came forward to receive him; nobody even spoke a word to him. Bhairab was not present there. After some time he came out on some business and called out, 'I say Govinda-da...' Suddenly seeing Ramesh standing there in the middle of the courtyard he was terrified out of his wits as if he had just seen a ghost and immediately scampered away and disappeared into the house.

When Ramesh came out of Bhairab's place, his face wore a gloomy look and he felt as if he was numbed with bewilderment. Suddenly he heard someone calling from behind, 'Ramesh, my son!' He turned round and found Dinu coming along with rapid strides. He came nearer and said, 'Come, my son. Let's go home.'

Ramesh tried to force a smile on his lips.

While walking by Ramesh's side, Dinu said, 'The help that you gave Bhairab was more than his own parents would've given him. Everybody knows that, but we're all helpless. We've our own families to look after. Therefore to invite you... I hope you'll understand.... One can't really blame Bhairab. You're all modern town-bred young men.... You've no respect for the caste scruples.... I think you'll understand.... Moreover, his youngest daughter is almost twelve... he'll have to arrange her marriage after some time.... You know everything about our society... I'm sure you'll understand....'

Impatiently Ramesh replied, 'Yes, I do understand.'

Standing outside the main gate of Ramesh's house, Dinu, who was apparently satisfied with the result of his talk, continued, 'Of course you'll understand. After all, you're a sensible person. But how can one blame that Brahmin either?... We old people have our future life to think of...'

'Oh, yes, that's right', said Ramesh and hurriedly entered his house. It was now quite clear to him that he had been ostracized by the village community. His eyes burned with anger and insult. What hurt him most was that Bhairab could invite and heartily welcome Beni and Govinda of all men; and that the villagers, who knew the whole story, not only forgave Bhairab's utter ingratitude in not even inviting Ramesh in order to win the favour of the village elders, but also justified and praised what he did.

Ramesh slumped into a chair and heaved a deep sigh. 'Oh my God!' he said, 'how will these ungrateful people atone for their heinous sins! Oh God, will you be able to forgive them for this cruel insult?'

CHAPTER
15

It was not that Ramesh had no such apprehension, yet when Gopal Sarkar returned from the district headquarters in the evening the next day and informed Ramesh that Bhairab had actually betrayed him – that he had not appeared before the court on the due date and the case had been dismissed *ex parte* and the amount deposited by Ramesh had gone into the pockets of Beni and others, Ramesh was so greatly infuriated that a streak of uncontrollable anger passed from the sole of his feet to the tips of his hair like a flash of lightning. Ramesh had deposited the entire amount of the false loan on behalf of Bhairab in order to defeat their fraud and forgery. But having saved his own skin with the help of that money, that great sinner Bhairab had now made friends with Beni. This ingratitude which surpassed the insult of the previous day made Ramesh's head burn in anger. Suddenly he sprang up and rushed out, dressed as he was. It did not even occur to him that he should control himself. Terrified by his angry looks, Gopal asked, 'Are you going out anywhere, Sir?'

'I'll be back in a minute', said Ramesh, and strode off.

When Ramesh arrived at Bhairab's house, there was no one in the outer rooms. So Ramesh entered the inner courtyard. Bhairab's wife was going to place the evening lamp at the foot of the sacred basil. Suddenly seeing Ramesh standing in front of her, she shrank back from him. As she remembered that this man had never before come to this house and guessed the reason for his coming that evening, she was completely petrified with fear.

Ramesh asked her, 'Where's Mr. Acharjya ?' The woman mumbled something indistinctly, but not a word of it was intelligible. However, it became clear that Bhairab was not at home. Ramesh had not even a shirt on him. His face also could not be seen clearly in the dim light of the evening. At that time Bhairab's eldest daughter, Lakshmi, came out with her son on her lap. Seeing a stranger standing there, she asked her mother, 'Who's he ?'

Her mother was much too scared to say anything. Ramesh also remained silent. Lakshmi was frightened and called, 'Father, there's somebody here in the court-yard; he doesn't speak!'

'Who's there?' shouted her father and came out of the room. Even in the darkness of the evening he could recognize that tall and straight figure. It made his blood freeze in terror.

Ramesh said strictly, 'Come here!' and immediately he himself went up to Bhairab and caught hold of one of his hands in an iron grip. He then thundered, 'Tell me why you've done this.'

Bhairab yelled. 'He's going to kill me, Lakshmi! Inform Beni Babu!' Immediately all the children set up a loud and piteous wail. In an instant their united screams rent the stillness of the evening sky and startled the entire neighbourhood.

Ramesh shook Bhairab violently and shouted, 'Shut up ! Tell me why you've done this.'

Bhairab didn't even attempt to answer him, but went on crying himself hoarse and tried to free himself from Ramesh's grip.

Soon the courtyard was crowded with inquisitive men and women from the neighbourhood. In order to enjoy the fun many assembled near the house and tried to push their way into the courtyard. But, blinded with

111

rage, Ramesh paid no heed to them. Like one insane, he went on shaking Bhairab violently, before the eyes of all the inquisitive spectators. A grossly exaggerated story of Ramesh's physical strength had already become a legend in the village. His fierce look terrified everybody and none among the crowd had the courage to come forward to extricate Bhairab. No sooner had Govinda Ganguly appeared on the scene than he melted away in the crowd. Beni peeped at Bhairab from a distance and was slipping away when Bhairab saw him and cried, 'Beni Babu ! Beni Babu !' But Beni Babu turned a deaf ear to his cries and disappeared somewhere in the twinkling of an eye.

Suddenly something like a passage was cleared through the crowd and the next moment Rama appeared. She came quickly and catching hold of Ramesh's hands said, 'That's enough, let him go!'

Ramesh cast a fiery look at her and demanded, 'Why?'

Rama clenched her teeth and said in an indistinct and angry tone, 'Doesn't it make you ashamed of your behaviour in the presence of so many persons ? It fills me with great shame.'

Ramesh now looked around at the crowd assembled in the courtyard and immediately released Bhairab. Rama then said in a low voice as before, 'Now go home.'

Without a word, Ramesh went away.

The whole thing appeared to be as amazing as magic. After Ramesh's departure, his unquestioning obedience to Rama attracted the people's notice and they began to look at each other meaningfully. The spectators seemed to be greatly disappointed that the affair which had started with such fanfare should have ended in such a tame and colourless manner.

The crowd slowly dispersed. Govinda now came over there and raising a finger, said with excessive gravity, 'You should now decide what action should be taken for this unlawful trespass and merciless assault.'

112

Bhairab was still panting, with his two knees pressed against his chest. He stared helplessly at Beni. Rama was still there. Guessing Beni's intended move, she said quickly, 'But Dada, Mr. Acharjya was also very much at fault. Besides, what has happened that we should make a fuss about it ?'

Greatly surprised, Beni remarked, 'What d'you say, Rama !'

Bhairab's eldest daughter was sobbing, leaning against a wooden post. She rasped and hissed like a serpent trampled underfoot. 'No wonder that you should plead for him, Rama Didi ! What would you've done if someone trespassed upon your house and beat up your father ?'

Rama was at first startled by Lakshmi's shout. Not only was the woman completely ungrateful for her father's release – however, that could possibly be ignored at the moment – but there was also something nastily taunting in her words which irritated Rama. She flared up in anger, but restrained herself and said, 'Well, Lakshmi, there's a lot of difference between your father and mine; they can't be compared. But I didn't say anything in support of anybody. What I said was for your good.'

Lakshmi was a village girl and an adept at quarrelling. She came forward in a threatening posture and rasped, 'Is that so ? Aren't you ashamed to be thus wrangling for his sake ? Nobody says anything out of fear, because you're a rich man's daughter; otherwise who hasn't heard about it ? It's because you are you that you show your face. Anybody else would've hanged herself !'

Beni reprimanded Lakshmi, 'You better keep quiet, Lakshmi. It's none of your business to talk of those things.'

'Why not?' retorted Lakshmi. 'Why should she squabble for the sake of the man who made father suffer so much ? What'd have happened if father had died ?'

Rama was only bewildered for a moment. But Beni's false show of anger inflamed her again. She gave Lakshmi a hard look and said, 'Lakshmi, it's a matter of merit for one to die in the hands of such a person! If your father had died today, he'd have gone straight to heaven.'

Lakshmi at once flared up, 'Oh! That's why you've welcomed death in his hands, Rama Didi!'

Rama did not say anything more to Lakshmi, but turning to Beni asked, 'What's that you're all hinting at, Dada?' She continued to stare at him with a fixed look. Her gaze seemed to penetrate through the darkness into the inner recesses of his mind.

Beni assumed an aggrieved tone and replied, 'How do I know? People talk of so many things... it's best you don't lend your ears to them.'

'But what do they talk about?'

Beni replied with feigned unconcern, 'Let them say whatever they like, Rama. After all their talk can't cause blisters on you!'

Rama saw through Beni's hypocritical sympathy. She remained silent for a moment and then said sharply, 'Well, nothing may cause blisters on your body. But everybody hasn't the thick skin of a rhinoceros that you have. But who's making people spread this scandal? Is it you?'

"I?"

Rama suppressed her uncontrollable rage with an effort and said, 'It's you, I'm sure; none else! You've already committed all sorts of crimes – theft, fraud, forgery, arson – why shouldn't you now indulge in scandal-mongering!'

Beni was too dazed to be able to say anything.

Rama went on, 'You're incapable of understanding what grievous ruin it means to a woman. But how'll this scandal-mongering benefit you?'

Beni was visibly shaken. 'How can this be of any

114

benefit to me ? But if people find you coming out of Ramesh's house early in the morning – what can I do?'

Rama continued, without caring for his words, 'Well, I don't like to tell you anything more in the presence of so many people. But don't think, Dada, that I don't understand what's in your mind. But I tell you if I've to die, I won't leave you alive either !'

Bhairab's wife had so long been standing silently close by. She now came forward, took Rama's arm and said in a low voice from behind her veil, 'What's this madness, my dear ? Who doesn't know in this village what you are?' She then turned to her daughter. 'Lakshmi, don't spread such a scandal against a woman, being a woman yourself. God won't ever forgive you. Had you been the daughter of a true man, you'd have fully realized what service she has rendered to you all today.' She then dragged Rama into a room. Her cruel taunt against her husband and her impartial truthfulness caused embarrassment to everyone present and they all slipped away.

Whatever might have been the causes of this incident, and however serious they might have been, his disgraceful lack of self-restraint so embarrassed Ramesh's cultured and gentle mind that he could not bring himself to stir out of his house for two whole days. At the same time there was a silver lining in the dark cloud of his shame, something that flashed from time to time like lightning and illumined his heart with a touch of beauty and grace – he was conscious that of all persons Rama alone had come forward, of her own accord, to share his shame. This gave him some satisfaction in the midst of his embarrassment. While he was thinking of continuing his voluntary solitary confinement for a few days more so as to savour the painful sensation of sorrow mixed with pleasure, he had no idea – in fact he could not have even dreamt of it – that in the meantime someone outside was facing an incessant shower of humiliation and insult for his sake.

But he was not allowed to enjoy his solitary confinement any longer. His Muslim tenants from Pirpur came in the afternoon and invited him to attend the meeting of their Council of Village Elders. Ramesh had himself organized this meeting a few days ago. Therefore when he was informed that they had all assembled at the meeting and were waiting for Chhoto Babu, he had to go. The reason why he had proposed this meeting was as follows :

Ramesh's enquiries had revealed that in every village the majority of the farmers were poor. Many of them had no land of their own. They lived on others' land on payment of rent and lived by working as hired labour in others' fields. If there was no work for a few days, either because they were unable to work on account of illness or for any other reason, they had no other alternative but to starve, along with their families. His enquiries further revealed that at one time many of them had some property, but had lost everything in repayment of their loans. The terms for lending money were also severe. Moneylenders gave loan only to those who mortgaged their lands as security, and the rate of interest was very high. As a result, once a farmer incurred a loan either to defray expenses for any obligatory social function or in the years of drought or excessive rainfall, he was never able to free himself from indebtedness and had to approach his moneylender for a fresh loan every year. The condition was the same whether the debtor was a Hindu or a Muslim. This was because the moneylenders were mostly Hindus.

When Ramesh lived in a town, he had read some books on rural indebtedness. The impression formed by him from his study was now confirmed by his personal experience and enquiries in the villages. This upset him greatly. He had a lot of money lying idle in banks. He decided to free these helpless farmers from the clutches of moneylenders by investing his own money along with that collected from other sources. He started in right earnest but soon suffered a jolt out of the first one or two cases. He found that in most cases the farmers were not really as helpless or as deserving of help as he had imagined them to be. They were undoubtedly poor, resourceless and slow-witted, but they did not lag behind others in dishonesty and wickedness. They tried their best to avoid repayment of any loan if they could help it. In most cases they were neither straightforward nor honest. They were not ashamed of telling lies and knew how to cheat others. They were also in the habit of taking an undue interest in their neighbours' wives and daughters. It was difficult for men to secure suitable brides for themselves; yet there was a large number of widows of all ages in every village. The moral health of the people was thus depraved. There was of course a village community and it also exercised some amount of discipline. But the relation of the corrupt people with the community was the same as that between a thief and the police. At the same time they were also so much oppressed, weak, and poor that one could not afford to be angry with them and give up. Ramesh's attitude towards these people was like the attitude of a father to his rebellious and wayward son. That was why he had called this meeting of the Council of Village Elders in the new school building at Pirpur.

The haziness of the evening had now cleared up and the bright light of the moon on the tenth night spread its brilliance upon the open meadow. Ramesh stood looking through his window at the moonlit meadow. Though he was already dressed to leave for Pirpur, he could not tear himself away from this beautiful sight and lingered about in his room.

Just then Rama came and stood at the doorway. It was dark. Ramesh took her to be one of the maids and asked, 'What d'you want?'

117

'Are you going out somewhere ?'

Ramesh was startled. 'Is that you, Rama ? Why at this hour?'

Rama had good reason to have recourse to the darkness of the evening to come to Ramesh, but that was a long story. Rama could not make up her mind how to begin; so she remained silent for a while. Ramesh also could not say anything. After some time Rama asked, 'How's your health these days ?'

'I'm not very well. In addition, I have fever every night.'

'Then you should go away for some time for a change.'

'I know,' smiled Ramesh, 'but how can I go ?'

His smile annoyed Rama. 'You'll say that you're awfully busy, but what's there more important than your own health?'

Ramesh said with a smile as before, 'Well, I don't say that one's health is an unimportant thing, but a man may have work which is more important to him than his health. But perhaps you won't understand it, Rama.'

Rama shook her head. 'Nor do I want to. But you must go somewhere. Leave necessary instructions with Mr. Sarkar that I'll look after the affairs of your estate.'

Ramesh was surprised. 'You'll look after the affairs of my estate ! But...'

'But what ?'

'But do you think I'll be able to trust you ?'

Rama replied at once, unhesitatingly, 'Common people may not, but you can.'

Her firm and inconceivable reply astonished Ramesh. After a brief silence he said, 'All right, I'll think about it.'

Rama shook her head, 'No, there's no time for leisurely thoughts. You've to go off somewhere this very night. Otherwise...'

Suddenly, she stopped. It became clear to her that from what she had already said, Ramesh was getting agitated, because it was not difficult for him to guess what might happen to him if he did not flee at once. Ramesh guessed correctly. He checked himself and said, 'Suppose I agree to run away as you suggest, how'll that benefit you? You've yourself tried your best to put me to trouble; then what's the point of cautioning me against a new danger? Those incidents aren't so old that you've entirely forgotten them. Better tell me frankly how my going away will benefit you. I might then agree to go.'

He continued looking at Rama's face, expecting a reply. But he got none.

Ramesh had not the faintest idea how deeply his words had wounded Rama. Nor was he able to see from her face, which was covered in darkness, how his cruel taunt had distressed her. Rama kept quiet for some time, trying to recover from the shock, and then said, 'All right, I'll be frank. If you don't, I'll be ruined. I'll have to bear witness against you.'

Ramesh said, drily, 'Oh, I see. But supposing you don't do so?'

Rama replied, after a while, 'In that case, nobody'll come to attend the Durga Puja in my house; nobody'll attend the banquet on the occasion of my brother Jatin's sacred thread ceremony or on the occasion of my other religious functions....' Rama shuddered even at the thought of such a catastrophe.

It was not necessary for Ramesh to hear anything more, but he could not restrain himself and asked, 'Then?'

'Need I tell you anything more?' cried Rama, greatly disconcerted. 'No, Ramesh-da, I entreat you, please go away immediately! Don't ruin me completely! Please go away from this place.... Go away at once!'

Both remained silent for some time. Previously whenever Ramesh met Rama anywhere, he would be in a flutter and the blood would race through his veins. He would argue with himself, reproach himself bitterly and yet he would find it impossible to calm himself. The silent revolt of his heart used to pain him, shame him, and anger him; but he was unable to control himself. Rama's sudden and unexpected appearance in his room all alone, this evening, so soon after the previous day's occurrence, had made his heart flutter more violently than ever. But Rama's last words set his heart at rest at long last, once for all. Rama's insistence on his going away only helped to reveal her utter selfishness in such a lurid light that it opened even his love-blinded eyes.

Ramesh drew a deep breath. 'All right, I'll go away,' he said. 'But there's no time tonight. Because however important my going away may be to you, this night is much more important to me. I've to go out immediately. Please call your maid.'

Rama said quietly, 'Isn't it at all possible for you to go away tonight ?'

'No, where's your maid ?'

'Nobody has come with me.'

'How's that !' said Ramesh, in surprise. 'How did you dare to come here all alone ! You haven't even brought a maid with you !'

'What's the use?' said Rama, as softly as before. 'She also couldn't have saved me from your hands.'

'Perhaps not ! But she'd have saved you at least from the wagging tongues of the scandal-mongers. It's getting late, Rani.'

'Rani' — that long-forgotten name with all the past memories !

Rama was on the point of saying, 'There has already been enough of it, Ramesh-da.' But she restrained herself and said instead, 'Even that wouldn't have been of any use, Ramesh-da. However, the night isn't dark. I can manage to go alone.'

Without waiting for another word, she left quietly.

CHAPTER
16

Rama celebrated the Durga Puja every year, in a big way. On the first day of the worship all the peasants and other poor people of the village were fed to their heart's content. There was always a scramble for a share of the consecrated food, and there was a regular crowd in the house till the end of the first quarter of the night. The entire outer courtyard would be littered with used up leaf-plates, earthen cups, leavings, etc., which would make free passage difficult. Not only the Hindus, but also the Muslim tenants of Pirpur came in large numbers to partake of the consecrated food.

Although Rama had been ill for some time now, arrangements for the festival were made on the usual scale. The image of Goddess Durga and her companion gods and goddesses were placed in the House of Worship, along with the necessary paraphernalia. Below it was the spacious courtyard, where the festivities were held.

The first day's worship was over in time. The midday had passed on to the afternoon, and the afternoon into the evening. The crescent moon of the seventh night appeared in the sky. And yet the vast courtyard of the Mukharji house was nearly deserted except for a few gentlemen. Inside the house, the huge heap of cooked rice turned cold and hard and the curry dried up and lost its colour. Still, not a single person had come to partake of the holy food.

Hookah in hand, Beni was stamping about, both

inside and outside the house, shouting angrily. "Ugh, these low-born fellows ! They've the audacity to spoil so much food ! I'll teach these rascals a good lesson !' he yelled. 'I'll demolish their roofs and drive them away from the village !' He continued to hurl threats saying he would do this and he would do that. Govinda, Dharmadas, Haldar and others also stamped about in rage trying to figure out who was the rascal responsible for this boycott. The strangest thing was that the Hindus and the Muslims had joined hands. Inside the house Rama's aunt was creating a scene – shouting, cursing, and crying – it was a virtual riot ! In the midst of all this commotion only one person was silent – Rama herself. She hadn't spoken a word against anybody nor blamed anyone – not a single word of complaint or of regret had escaped her lips. Was this the same Rama? She was undoubtedly very ill – although she would never admit it and laughed away the suggestion. Illness spoils beauty – that was a different thing: but she had none of her old pride, anger and obstinacy. Her two lacklustre eyes seemed full of sorrow and compassion. Yet if one looked a little carefully, one would notice that behind those two moist eyes was hidden a sea of tears which, if it was allowed to come out, would flood the world.

Rama came into the House of Worship through the back door and stood by the side of the image of Goddess Durga. As soon as her well-wishers saw her, they began to shout abuses and curses against the low-born people. Rama did not say anything, she simply smiled – the smile of a flower torn from its stem and held by a human hand. It did not express anger or malice, hope or despair, weal or woe. Who knows whether that smile had any significance or not?

Beni burst out angrily, 'No, no, it's not a matter to be laughed at ! It's a very serious matter! Once I come to know who is at the root of this – (he put the nails of his two hands together) – I'll tear him to pieces like this !'

Rama shuddered. Beni went on: 'You bastards ! You don't realize that the man who made you so arrogant is himself now in jail, doing hard labour! How long will it take me to finish you off!'

Rama did not say a word. When the work for which she had come was over, she silently went away.

Ramesh was now in jail for the last one and a half months on the charge of unlawful trespass upon Bhairab's house, and assault on him. The prosecution didn't have much difficulty in proving the charge. The new magistrate, who tried the case, observed that he had received prior information that such a crime was possible and natural for the accused. He even had his misgivings whether the accused was not implicated in other crimes like armed robbery. He received valuable help from the records of the police station, which disclosed that the accused had committed similar criminal offences before, and that his name was mentioned in connection with many kinds of suspicious activities. The magistrate even suggested, in course of his judgment, that the police should keep a watchful eye on the accused in future. Although it was not necessary for the prosecution to cite many witnesses, Rama had to give evidence. In her deposition she said that she knew Ramesh had entered Bhairab's house to assault him, but did not know whether he had actually stabbed Bhairab or not. Nor could she remember whether he had a knife in his hand.

Was this the truth? Rama had made this statement on oath in the court of the District Magistrate. But what reply would she give in that court where one is not required to make an oath ? Who knew better than she that Ramesh had not stabbed Bhairab, and that he did not have even a blade of grass in his hand, let alone a weapon ! In that court nobody would ask her what she could remember and what she could not. But she had no

123

chance of speaking the truth in this court. The village
community, under the thumb of Beni and his associates,
did not want that she should speak the truth. She had no
doubt in her mind that if she had the temerity to defy
them and speak the truth in the court, they would not
hesitate to besmirch her fair name with the black hue of
scandal and excommunicate her from society. Such
cases were not rare. Moreover, Rama had never imagined even in her wildest dreams that the punishment
would be so severe. She had thought that at the worst
Ramesh would be fined a sum of one or two hundred
rupees. When Ramesh had disregarded her repeated
warnings and not agreed to run away leaving his work,
she, in her anger, had even wished that he should be
punished with a fine so that he would learn a lesson. But
she had never thought that the lesson could be so harsh
as this; that the court would not take into consideration
his pale and emaciated face and would sentence him to
six months' rigorous imprisonment, without showing
any mercy to him. When the judgment was delivered,
Rama did not have the heart to look up at Ramesh's face.
Later, she was told by others that Ramesh had kept on
gazing at her steadily all the time and had not allowed
anyone to cross-examine her. When Gopal Sarkar proposed to file an appeal against the order of his conviction, Ramesh had shaken his head and said, 'No! Even
if the magistrate were to sentence me to life imprisonment, I wouldn't like to lodge an appeal for obtaining
acquittal. I think even jail is better than that.'

Quite so. When the ever-loyal Bhairab Acharjya could
repay his debt by bringing a false charge against him
and when Rama, standing in the witness box, could not
remember whether Ramesh had a knife in his hand,
what was the point of making an appeal for release! The
intense feeling of hurt which Ramesh sustained settled
like a massive slab of stone upon Rama's heart and
weighed it down with remorse; she was unable to put it

away. Her reasoning that she had not told a lie in the court was not accepted by the all-knowing God who lived in her heart. It was a fact that she had not told a lie, but at the same time she had not disclosed the truth either. If only she knew that suppression of truth was such a great offence and she would burn and smart under it forever ! From time to time she remembered how grievous Bhairab's wrongs were which had forced Ramesh to lose self-control. Yet her one request had made him forgive Bhairab and he had gone away without so much as a word. Who else had ever obeyed her wishes so submissively and honoured her so greatly ?

The constant remorse and repentance seemed to have at last given Rama an insight into the truth. She had committed such a reprehensible act because of her fear of the village community. But where was that community? Did it exist anywhere outside the selfishness and malice of a few leaders like Beni and his henchmen ? Who in this village was ignorant of Beni's affairs with the widow of Govinda's brother ? And yet that woman was safely enjoying the protection of the community and the same Beni was its leader. It was strange that everyone felt gratified to be bound by the shackles of discipline imposed by such a community ! This was Hinduism in practice ! When Rama thought of her own conduct, she felt she could not be angry even with Bhairab who was at the root of all her troubles. His younger daughter was already twelve. If she were not given in marriage soon, Bhairab would be excommunicated from the society and his family would become outcastes. The mere apprehension of such a calamity was enough to unnerve a Hindu and his heart would quail at the very thought of it. Despite all her advantages if she could not shake off her fear of the community, how could poor Bhairab afford to do so? She could not deny that it would be ruinous for Bhairab to go against Beni.

Old Sanatan Hajra was passing by the road in front of

Rama's house. Seeing him, Govinda called out, entreated him, and at last practically dragged him up to Beni. The latter blurted out angrily, 'Since when have you people become so arrogant, Sanatan ? Have you grown another head on your shoulders ?'

'Who ever has two heads, Babu? When you gentlemen don't have more than one head, how could we poor people have two?'

'What did you say?' roared Beni, and then fell silent. His anger was so great that it made him speechless. Sometime ago when this Sanatan's entire landed property was mortgaged to Beni, he would come twice a day and grovel at Beni's feet. The same Sanatan had now the impudence to speak in this manner !

Govinda said sarcastically, 'We're merely watching your nerve, Sanatan. None of you came to partake of even the consecrated food. Tell me, what's at the root of all this?'

The old man smiled sadly and said, 'How can I have any nerve, Sir? You've already ruined me, haven't you? Forget it. But whether it is food offered to Goddess Durga or anything else, no fisherman will henceforth come to a Brahmin's house for a meal. We wonder how Mother Earth can be permitting so much sin.' He sighed and then turned to Rama. 'Do take care, Young Mistress. The Muslim youth of Pirpur are mad with rage. Only Mother Durga knows what'll happen when Chhoto Babu is released from jail. They've already prowled round Beni Babu's house twice or thrice... he's lucky they didn't get him!' Saying this he looked at Beni. In an instant Beni's angry face turned deathly pale in terror.

'I'm not telling a lie in front of the Goddess, Babu,' said Sanatan. 'Please be careful and don't go out after nightfall. Nobody knows where they may be lying in wait for you.'

Beni wanted to say something, but no sound passed through his lips. There was not probably a greater coward in the world.

Rama now broke her silence and said, sadly and tenderly, 'Sanatan, are you all angry because of Chhoto Babu?'

Sanatan looked at the image of the Goddess Durga and then said, 'Yes, dear Didi, that's the reason. Why should I tell you a lie and be cast into hell? The Muslims bear the severest grudge. They regard Chhoto Babu as a Prophet of the Hindus.... I'll give you an example. Jafar Ali, that close-fisted miser, who never parted with as much as a pice, donated one thousand rupees for their school on the day of Chhoto Babu's imprisonment. I'm told that they even offer prayers in their mosques invoking the blessing of Allah on Chhoto Babu.'

Rama's sad and pale face lit up with unspoken joy. Silently she went on gazing at Sanatan with bright and steady eyes.

Beni grasped Sanatan's hands abruptly and said, 'Sanatan, you must go and report this to the Sub-Inspector of Police. I'll give you whatever you want. I'll even release two bighas of your land if you ask for it. I swear in the presence of the deity! Please accede to a Brahmin's request!'

Sanatan stared at Beni for some time, in utter amazement, and then said, 'How long am I going to live, Babu, that I should give in to such temptation? If I do that, when I die nobody will even touch my body with his foot, not to speak of carrying it to the cremation ground. Those old days are gone, Babu, gone for ever! Chhoto Babu has changed everything.'

Govinda interposed, 'Then you won't keep a Brahmin's request?'

Sanatan shook his head. 'No. You may be angry with me, Mr. Ganguly, for saying this. But Chhoto Babu told us at the meeting held in the new school building at Pirpur, "No one becomes a Brahmin simply because he has a few threads hanging down his shoulder". Well,

Sir, I'm not a child of yesterday. I know everything. What you go about doing – is that befitting a Brahmin? What d'you say, young Mistress ?'

Rama silently hung down her head. Encouraged at their silence, Sanatan now went on, as if to wreak vengeance, 'The most aggressive are the youths. Every evening all the young men of the two villages meet at Jafar Ali's house. They're openly saying, "Chhoto Babu's the only man whom we regard as our landowner. The others are all rogues – thieves and cut-throats. Besides, we pay rent on our land. Then why should we be afraid of anybody ? And, if one acts like a true Brahmin, then only shall we regard him as a Brahmin. Otherwise they're just like us." '

Terrified out of his wits, Beni asked with a pale face, "Well, Sanatan, why are they so very angry with me of all people ?"

'Don't take it amiss, Babu,' replied Sanatan, 'but everyone knows that you're the villain of the piece.'

Beni fell silent. Even such an accusation by a low-born fellow like Sanatan failed to anger him, because he was much too terrified even to become angry. His heart throbbed violently.

Govinda said, 'Oh, so they're having their rendezvous at Jafar Ali's house, is it? Can you tell us what they do there?'

Sanatan looked into Govinda's face and thought for a moment, and then said, 'I don't know for certain. But I warn you, Mister, if you wish yourself well, give up your evil plans. The Hindus and the Muslims are treating each other as brothers – they're all united, they're of one mind and one purpose. Since the day of Chhoto Babu's imprisonment, in their anger they've become as inflammable as gunpowder. For Heaven's sake, don't strike a spark there – it'll lead to a conflagration !'

Sanatan went away. For quite some time nobody was in a mood to speak. When Rama got up to go in, Beni said, 'Have you noted what Sanatan said ?'

An amused smile played on Rama's face, but she said nothing. Her smile irritated Beni. He said, 'That rascal Bhairab is responsible for all this. Besides, nothing would've happened if you hadn't gone there and set him free from Ramesh's grip. You can afford to smile, because you're a woman and it's not necessary for you to go out. But what will happen to us ? What if one of them really breaks my head one of these days? This is what happens when you work with a woman!' Overcome with fear, anger, and sorrow, Beni fell silent with a scowl on his face.

Rama was flabbergasted. She knew Beni's nature very well. But she didn't expect such a shameless and perverse accusation even from him. She remained standing for a while without a word, and then went away. Beni then began to shout for torches and an escort, and when these were arranged, he left accompanied by five or six persons and two or three torches and went on his way with rapid, frightened steps, looking around with apprehensive eyes.

CHAPTER
17

Bishweshwari entered the room and said in a voice choked with tears, 'How are you today, daughter?'

Rama looked at her face with a faint smile and said, 'I'm better today, Aunty.'

Bishweshwari sat at the head of the bed and silently stroked her head and face. For the past three months Rama had been confined to her bed, suffering from the pernicious effects of chronic malaria and persistent cough. The old village Ayurvedic doctor was trying his best to cure her, though unsuccessfully. The poor old man did not know what the real malady was which was eating into her vitals every moment. Bishweshwari alone had a suspicion in her mind which was gradually growing stronger. She loved Rama like her own daughter – it was true love – and this gave her vision an exceptional keenness to discover the truth. When others, in their mistaken notion, made wrong diagnoses and prescribed wrong medicines and gave false hope, her heart seemed to be breaking. She noticed that while Rama's eyes had sunk deep into their sockets, their look was very keen, as if Rama earnestly wished to see at close quarters something which was at a great distance. She asked softly, 'Rama?'

'Yes, Aunty.'

'I am like your mother, aren't I?'

Rama interposed, 'Why "like", Aunty? You *are* indeed my mother.'

Bishweshwari lowered her face and kissed Rama's

130

forehead. 'Then tell me the truth, daughter. Tell me what's really the matter with you.'

'I'm ill, Aunty.'

Bishweshwari noticed that for a moment Rama's extremely pale face had turned crimson. With deep affection she stroked Rama's dishevelled hair and caressed her.

'That I can see with my naked eyes, dear. But if there's anything which can't be seen with ordinary eyes, don't hide it from your mother. Otherwise how can you be cured?'

Outside, the morning sun had not yet grown warm. A cool gentle breeze was blowing – the first indications of the oncoming winter. Rama, who was looking out of the window, remained silent. After some time she asked, 'How's Dada, Aunty?'

'He's better', said Bishweshwari. 'Of course it'll take some time before the wound on his head heals completely, but he should be able to come from the hospital in five or six days.'

Noticing a sign of anguish on Rama's face, Bishweshwari said, 'Don't feel sorry, my child. He needed it. It'll do him good.' Seeing that Rama looked surprised, Bishweshwari added, 'You're wondering how I, his mother, can say this after he was so seriously wounded. But believe me, my dear, I don't know whether this incident has pained me more than it has pleased me. I know that those, who aren't afraid of sin or shame, must at least be afraid of their death; otherwise this world would go to rack and ruin. So I think that the oilman's son, who assaulted Beni, did him such a good turn, that no friend or relative of his could even do the same. You can't change the black hue of coal by merely washing it; you've to burn it in fire.'

'Was there nobody at home at that time?' asked Rama.

'Why not? Everybody was there. The man didn't do it on the spur of the moment, he did it deliberately. He was

131

fully prepared to go to jail when he came to sell oil. He had no personal vendetta. So when Beni fell unconscious at the very first blow of his pole, he quietly remained standing... he didn't hit Beni again. But before he left, he gave a serious warning that if Beni didn't mend his ways, this wasn't the last time that he'd be assaulted, no matter whether he himself came back alive from jail or not.'

'That means there are other people behind him,' said Rama slowly. 'But the low-born people in our part of the country were never so bold as this before, I wonder where they got their courage from?'

Bishweshwari smiled, 'Don't you know, my child, who has filled their hearts with strength ? When a fire breaks out, it doesn't go out by itself; even when it's put out, it leaves some of its heat within the things around it. After Ramesh comes back from jail, he may live wherever he likes – may God grant him a long life ! – but I shall never sigh in sorrow for Beni's sake.'

Rama perceived that in spite of what Bishweshwari had just said, she did suppress a sigh with an effort. Rama took Bishweshwari's hand in hers, put it on her bosom, and kept quiet.

After she had recovered her composure, Bishweshwari added, 'Only a mother knows what it means to have an only child. I can't tell you how I felt when they carried Beni in an unconscious state, placed him into the carriage and removed him to the hospital. Yet let alone curse, I couldn't even blame anybody. I couldn't forget that a mother's love for her son wouldn't stay the hands of God from inflicting punishment on the guilty.'

Rama thought for a while and said, 'I'm not arguing with you, Aunty, but if God's punishment is so inexorable, which sin is Ramesh-da expiating? Everyone knows how we conspired to put him into jail.'

'Yes, they know. And that's why Beni's in hospital now, and you...' She suddenly stopped and swallowed

132

the words which were at the tip of her tongue. Then she continued, 'You see, no action disappears in vain, without producing some effect somewhere. Its power is sure to produce some result somewhere. But how it works its way is not always obvious. That's why it hasn't yet been possible to solve this problem why one has to expiate the sins committed by another. But there's not the least doubt that sometimes one has to suffer for another's sin.'

Rama remembered her own part in the drama and drew a long breath, as quietly as she could. Bishweshwari went on, 'This episode has opened my eyes too, Rama. You can't always do good to others simply because you want to. One must have the patience to climb a flight of stairs in the beginning. One day Ramesh came to me, utterly despondent. "Aunty, let me stop trying to do good to these people and go back to where I came from", he said. I prevented him from going away; "No, Ramesh, if you have started some work, don't abandon it and run away", I said. He cannot disobey me, and so he stayed on. Therefore when I heard about his imprisonment, I felt as if it was I who had bound him hand and foot and inflicted this punishment on him. But later, on the day when Beni was removed to the hospital, it occurred to me that it was also necessary for Ramesh to undergo this term of imprisonment. I hadn't known before that it was so difficult for one, who had come from outside, to do good to the people. It didn't occur to me at all that, first of all, he must be one with the people he wants to serve – both in their good as well as bad. From the very beginning Ramesh stood on so high a pedestal – with his education, culture, great physical strength, and large heart – that no one could reach up to him. But it escaped my notice. I didn't allow him to go, but at the same time I couldn't keep him with us.'

Rama was going to say something, but checked herself. Bishweshwari guessed what Rama wanted to say.

133

'No, Rama, I don't repent that,' she said. 'Please don't be cross with me, my child, but I can confidently tell you that now that you people have dragged him down to your own level and made him a part of it, however unrighteous that act may have been, he'll be able to find the real truth after his return from jail.'

Rama wasn't able to follow her. 'But why should Ramesh-da come down, Aunty? However bitter may be his sufferings as a result of our sinful acts, our misdeeds should pull us alone down the path of hell... why should they touch him?'

Bishweshwari smiled sadly, 'Of course, they'll! Otherwise sin wouldn't have been so horrible. If one's not grateful to one's benefactor for all his help, but on the contrary, harms him, it does not matter much, unless such ingratitude pulls down the benefactor as well. Do you think Ramesh'll be the same man when he comes back to Kuanpur? No, my dear. Soon it'll be clear to you all that Ramesh's right hand, with which he used to give charity freely, has been twisted and broken by Bhairab.'

Bishweshwari continued after a pause, 'But who knows? Perhaps, after all, it has been just as well. As the villagers weren't fit for the abundant gifts from his powerful and able hand, his disabled hand'll perhaps prove much more useful to them.' She heaved a deep sigh.

Rama silently stroked Bishweshwari's hand for some time and then asked, slowly, in a pathetic voice, 'Aunty, what's the punishment for giving false evidence and sending an innocent man to jail?'

Bishweshwari looked out through the open window and went on running her fingers through Rama's dishevelled hair. Suddenly she noticed that tears were streaming out of Rama's closed eyes. She wiped the tears affectionately, and said, 'But you had no choice in this matter, my child. Those cowards who intimidated you into submission with their threats to spread scandals against you are the ones who are guilty, and all the punishment will fall on their heads. You won't have to suffer any punishment.' She wiped Rama's tears again. These comforting words opened the floodgates of Rama's tears which now gushed out like a spring and began to fall in torrents. After some time she said, 'But they're after all his enemies. They say that there's no sin in liquidating an enemy by hook or by crook. But in my case, I've no such excuse, Aunty.'

'Why haven't you such an excuse, dear ?' asked Bishweshwari. But so soon as she lowered her face after putting this question, truth revealed itself to her like a sudden flash of lightning. The suspicion which had been flitting through her mind for some time now seemed at last to have cast off its mask. Bishweshwari was overwhelmed with a profound sense of sorrow and surprise. At last she knew the reason for Rama's broken heart.

Rama's eyes were closed; so she could not see the changed expression on Bishweshwari's face. She called, 'Aunty !'

Bishweshwari was startled. She responded with a nod of her head.

Rama said, 'Aunty, I've a confession to make to you today. The young men who met at Jafar Ali's house at Pirpur every evening, used to discuss various measures for the good of the village in accordance with Rameshda's instructions. A plot was hatched to send a report to the police to the effect that these young men were a band of ruffians. Of course that's what the police wanted. Once they caught hold of these boys, there would've been no end to their harassment. So I sent word to warn them.'

Bishweshwari shuddered, 'Oh dear!' she exclaimed. 'Beni wanted to invite such trouble from the police into his own village for nothing!'

'I think Dada's assault was the result of this development,' said Rama. 'Will you be able to forgive me, Aunty?'

Bishweshwari bent her head and kissed Rama's forehead. 'If I can't forgive you being his mother, who else can?' she said. 'Rather I pray to God that he may bless you for this good act of yours.'

Rama wiped the tears from her eyes with her hand and said, 'I've only one consolation, Aunty. When he comes back from jail, he'll be glad to see that his field of activities is ready. What he wanted has happened – the peasants and other poor people have at last risen from their long stupor – they've accepted him as their friend and given him their love. This'll undoubtedly give him immense pleasure. In the midst of his great joy won't he be able to forgive my guilt, Aunty?'

Bishweshwari was too deeply moved to say anything. Only a big drop of tear rolled down her cheeks on to Rama's forehead. Then both remained silent for a long time.

'Aunty?'

'Yes, my child.'

'Only in one thing the two of us couldn't remain separated – we both loved you dearly.'

Bishweshwari again bent down and kissed Rama's forehead.

'On the strength of that love, I'll make one request to you today, Aunty. If he's not able to forgive me even when I'm no more, please tell him on my behalf that I wasn't really so bad as he knew me to be, and whatever suffering I might've caused him, I've suffered much more myself. I hope he won't disbelieve this when he hears it from you.'

Bishweshwari embraced Rama and pressing her to her bosom, burst into tears. 'Let's go to some place of pilgrimage', she sobbed, 'where there's no Beni and no Ramesh, where one can see the spire of the temple of God as soon as one lifts one's eyes. Let's go to such a place, Rama. I've understood everything. If your end isn't far, my child, you've to get rid of this canker which is eating into your heart. We're daughters of Brahmins; when the time comes for us to cross over to the other bank, we must go in a manner befitting us.'

Rama remained silent for a long time. Then, controlling a deep sigh, she said, 'I also want to go that way, Aunty.'

CHAPTER
18

Ramesh couldn't possibly hope, even in his wildest
dreams, that outside the prison walls God had arranged
to transmute all his sufferings into such satisfaction.
When he stepped out of the jail gate at the end of his six-
month term, he saw something inconceivable. At the
head of a procession was Beni Ghoshal himself, with a
wrap round his head. Behind him were the teachers and
students of the two schools and some Hindu and Muslim
tenants. Beni gave Ramesh a warm hug and said in a
choked voice, 'Ramesh, my brother, I've at last realized
the strength of the bond of love for one's nearest kin. I
knew that Jadu Mukharji's daughter might win over
that bastard Acharjya and then throwing shame to the
winds, appear in the court and give false evidence
against you in order to get you into trouble, yet I didn't
forestall the move in time. God has punished me suita-
bly for my neglect. I must say you were much better off
inside the jail. I passed these six months in great
remorse as if burning in a slow fire of husks.'

Ramesh did not know what to do or say and was bewildered. Mr. Parui, the headmaster of Kuanpur school,
prostrated himself before Ramesh and took the dust
from his feet. Those who were behind him now came
forward one by one and greeted Ramesh appropriately
– with blessings or salaam or obeisance. Ramesh was
virtually mobbed. Beni now burst into tears and said in
a choked voice, 'Ramesh, my dear, please forget the past
and don't be angry with your brother any longer. Let's
go home to mother. She's been crying her eyes out.'

A hackney carriage had been kept ready. Ramesh boarded it without a word. Beni took the seat opposite him and removed the wrap from his head. Although the wound had healed, the scar still showed. Beni heaved a deep sigh and turning his right palm out said, 'Who shall I blame ? This was my fate... the result of my own sins ! But why must you hear that story? 'He assumed an expression of deep sorrow on his face and fell silent. Beni's frank confession touched Ramesh's heart. He thought that something unpleasant must have happened in the meantime. So he did not press for details. But Beni became restless, as he noticed that the purpose for which he had introduced this topic was ending up in smoke. After remaining silent for a while, he again tried to attract Ramesh's attention with a deep sigh and said slowly, 'Since my childhood, I've been handicapped by one bad habit – I can't practise duplicity, and because I can't hide my feelings like others, I've had to suffer grievously. Still I don't seem to be able to come to my senses.'

Noticing that Ramesh was listening to him silently, Beni lowered his voice and said, gravely, 'My only fault was that I couldn't suppress my anguish any longer and told her with tears in my eyes, "Rama, what harm did we two brothers do to you that you punished us in this way? If mother comes to know that Ramesh has been jailed, she'll give up her life. Ramesh and I may go on fighting between ourselves over the estate, yet he's my own brother. By one single stroke you've killed my brother and my mother both ! However, God will protect the innocent."' Saying this Beni looked towards the sky through the open door of the carriage as if to lodge another complaint.

Ramesh did not join Beni in this complaint, but he listened attentively. After a pause Beni continued, 'I still shudder to think how terrible and fierce she looked. Clenching her teeth, she said with fury, "Didn't

Ramesh's father try to send my father to jail? Would he have spared my father if he succeeded in his attempt ?" I couldn't tolerate this woman's bluster any longer. So I lost my temper and said, "All right, let him come back. We'll then take appropriate measures.'"

Till now, Ramesh was unable to follow clearly what Beni was talking about. He did not know when his father had tried to send Rama's father to jail. But he now remembered that soon after his return to the village he had heard such an accusation from Rama's aunt. He was now eager to hear the rest of Beni's story.

Beni noticed this and added, 'She had previous experience of committing murder. She had sent Akbar, the fighter, to kill you... I'm sure you will remember it. But the trick didn't work with you. On the contrary, you taught her a good lesson. But the case was different with me. You see, I'm a weak and frail person....' Beni stopped, thought for a few moments and dug out of his black heart an imaginary account of his assault by the son of Tustu, the oilman.

Ramesh asked with bated breath, 'Then ?'

Beni smiled sadly and said, 'I don't remember what happened then! – who removed me to the hospital, how they carried me, what happened in the hospital, who looked after me there, I remember nothing. I regained consciousness after ten days and then I came to know that I was in the hospital. It's only as a result of my mother's piety that I was saved from sure death...who else is so lucky as to have such a mother as mine!'

Ramesh was unable to speak a word and remained rooted to his seat like a figure of wood, only the fingers of his hands clenched in a firm grip. It was not possible for anyone to gauge the intensity of the anger and hatred that had begun to blaze in his head like a flame. He knew very well how wicked Beni was. He was also aware that nothing was impossible for him. But he had not the experience to imagine that a man could utter so

140

much falsehood so unhesitatingly and so glibly. So Ramesh swallowed as truth all that Beni told him against Rama.

Ramesh's return to the village ushered in a series of festivities. Every day people came to greet him in the morning, at noon, and even at night and spoke to him so nicely and displayed such friendship, that whatever bitterness the imprisonment had left in his heart soon vanished. It was clear to Ramesh that during his absence there had been a social upheaval in the village. When he began to analyse how such a great change could have taken place in the course of these few months, he found that the stream of change, which was unable to make any headway due to Beni's obstruction and was at the same time silently gathering strength, had begun to flow with redoubled energy when it received Beni's support. For the first time Ramesh was able to comprehend Beni a little better. He now realized, as he had never done before, that although the villagers know Beni as a great evil-doer, yet they were most obedient to him. Spared this man's opposition, Ramesh heaved a sigh of relief. Not only this, one after another all the villagers came and expressed their deep sense of sorrow at the injustice done to Ramesh and the suffering caused to him. Their collective sympathy and Beni's co-operation filled Ramesh's heart with great pleasure and enthusiasm. He made up his mind to take up with redoubled enthusiasm all the projects which he had started six months ago and had left unfinished. He began to take part in the rejoicings of the villagers unhesitatingly and called on everyone, irrespective of their status, and enquired about their affairs.

But with constant effort he managed to keep himself completely aloof from only one matter – that was Rama's affairs. He had heard on his way to the village that she was ill, but had made no enquiries to find out how grave her illness was now. He had formed the impression that he had cut off all connection with her forever. After his return to the village he heard from the villagers that everyone knew that Rama alone was at the root of all his trouble. So he had no doubt in his mind that Beni had not told him a lie in this matter.

After five or six days Beni came to Ramesh and began to press him for his help in a matter concerning the partition of an important piece of landed property at Pirpur. He had a misunderstanding with Rama over this matter, but it had not yet come into the open. Beni wanted to take advantage of Rama's illness to grab that piece of property. Whatever he might say openly, Beni was at heart afraid of Rama. Now that she was confined to bed and was not in a position to go to court, and the Muslim tenants of Pirpur would not turn down a request made by Ramesh, this was the best opportunity to oust Rama and to take possession of the property. Whatever might happen in the future they must not miss this opportunity. This was Beni's argument and he began to press Ramesh to agree to his proposal. When Ramesh did not agree, Beni adduced many arguments in support of his proposal, and at last said, 'Why are you hesitant ? Did she ever spare you whenever she had an opportunity that you should take into consideration her illness? Were you in better health when she sent you to jail?' Ramesh could not deny that Beni's reasoning was correct. Yet he could not agree to go against Rama. In spite of Beni's persistent instigation, Ramesh could not be incited to take any action against Rama and when he remembered her illness and her helpless condition all his feeling of antagonism shrank and vanished from his mind. The reason for this was not quite clear even to himself. So Ramesh remained silent and did not commit himself. Whenever Beni felt that his arguments would produce the desired effect in due course, he knew how to be patient. So he preferred not to press any further for the time being and went away.

There was another thing which attracted Ramesh's notice this time. He had all along known that Bishweshwari did not have such attachment to worldly affairs. But he now felt that her non-attachment had in the meantime turned to aversion. On the day of his release from jail, when he came to her house, along with Beni, Bishweshwari had expressed her joy, and in her usual calm voice had showered blessings on him again and again, yet there was something missing which had pained him. Today someone told him casually that Bishweshwari would soon be leaving for Benares with the intention of living there for the rest of her life and would not come back to Kuanpur again. Ramesh was startled to hear this. How was it that he knew nothing about it ? It was true that he had not been able to make time to go and meet her in the past five or six days, in the midst of his multifarious activities. But Bishweshwari had not told him anything about it when he last met her. He knew that she never liked to talk about herself or others of her own accord, but the meaning of her total indifference to worldly affairs dawned on him when he placed his memory of the happenings of that day and the news which he had just heard side by side. He had not the least doubt now that Aunty was actually going to bid them goodbye for ever. When he thought what her absence would mean to him, his eyes filled with tears. Without wasting a minute he went straight to her.

It was then about nine or ten in the morning. As he was about to enter Aunty's room, a maid informed him that she was not at home and had gone to the Mukharji house. Ramesh was surprised. 'At such an odd hour?' he asked. The maid was an old employee of this house. She replied with a smile, 'No time is odd enough for her. Besides, the young master's sacred thread ceremony is taking place today.'

Jatin's sacred thread ceremony ! Ramesh was amazed at this news. He said, 'But nobody seems to know

143

anything about it?'

'They haven't invited anybody,' replied the maid. 'In any case no one would've gone to attend the ceremony, even if they were invited – Rama Didi has been excommunicated by the village elders.'

Ramesh's surprise knew no bounds. He kept quiet for a moment and then asked, 'But what's the reason for it?'

The maid turned her head aside with embarrassment, and said, 'I don't know for certain...but people talk all kinds of things about her....We're poor people, Chhoto Babu. What have we got to do with it?' Saying this she slipped away.

Ramesh remained silent for a while and then returned home. Even without enquiry he was convinced that this was Beni's cruel revenge against Rama. But he was not able to guess fully what the precise reason for Beni's anger was, what Rama's offence was for which he wanted to take this revenge, and what the nature of the scandal spread by him was.

CHAPTER
19

An event, thoroughly inconceivable in nature, took place that afternoon. Not caring for adjudication by the court, Kailash, the barber, and Sheikh Motilal came to Ramesh, accompanied by their respective witnesses, and sought his help for settling their dispute.

'Why should you accept my decision?' Ramesh asked, with genuine surprise.

Both the complainant and the defendant replied, 'Why not, Sir? Are you in any way less educated than the judge? Moreover, it's only educated gentlemen like you who become judges and magistrates. If you're appointed by the government as a judge tomorrow, and you decide our case, we'll be bound to abide by your decision. We can't then say that we aren't prepared to accept your verdict.'

This filled Ramesh's heart with delight and pride.

Kailash said, 'Sir, here we can argue our own case before you, but that's not possible in a court of law. Moreover, one who can't afford to pay a handsome fee to a lawyer doesn't get any advantage from a law court. Here we aren't required to spend even a pice. It's not necessary to engage a lawyer and wheedle him, and we won't have to move up and down all the way to the district headquarters a thousand and one times. No, Sir, whatever decision you may give, favourable or unfavourable, we'll abide by it; and after the case is decided, we shall bow down to you and go back happy. God was kind enough to give us the wisdom to withdraw our case from the court of law and seek your help in this matter.'

The dispute concerned a small water-course. They handed over to Ramesh whatever documents they had and went away with their witnesses, saying that they would be back on the next day.

Ramesh sat quietly for some time. He was exhilarated. This was something beyond his imagination. He had never hoped for such a development even in the distant future. These two persons might or might not abide by his decision, but the very fact that they had decided to settle their dispute out of court and had approached him for a decision gave him immense pleasure. It was not a big affair – just a petty dispute of two ordinary villagers – but he envisaged endless possibilities arising out of this petty case and began building castles in the air. It seemed to him that he had unlimited scope for serving this unhappy place of birth of his.

It was a night in spring. The open spaces all around seemed flooded in bright moonlight. Looking at it, absent-mindedly, Ramesh seemed to remember Rama. On other days this would have caused him immediate irritation; but tonight, not to speak of any irritation anywhere, there was not even a trace of annoyance in him. He smiled to himself and spoke, addressing the absent Rama, 'You certainly had no idea, Rama, that through you God would give me such success in life and that the poison administered by you would turn to nectar and sweeten my whole existence. Had you known this, perhaps you wouldn't have sent me to jail.... Who's there?'

'I'm Radha, Chhoto Babu. Rama Didi has earnestly requested you to come and see her just for once.'

Rama had sent a maid to call him! Ramesh was astounded. Who was this playful god making all sorts of queer jokes with him today ?

The maid reminded, 'Chhoto Babu, if you'd kindly...?'

'Where's she?

146

'Lying in bed.' After a pause she added. 'There won't be any time tomorrow, so if you'd kindly...'

'All right, I'm coming.' Ramesh rose to his feet, ready to go.

After she had sent her maid to call Ramesh, Rama lay on her bed in her room in a state of tension. When Ramesh entered the room shown by the maid and sat down on a chair, Rama pulled herself out of the bed with sheer will power and threw herself at Ramesh's feet. An oil lamp was burning feebly in one corner of the room. In its dim light Ramesh saw Rama indistinctly, but he could not realize how serious her illness was. On his way to this house, Ramesh had made many resolves in his mind. All of them lost their edge in Rama's presence. After keeping quiet for a while, Ramesh asked gently, 'How are you now, Rani?'

Rama moved a little away from Ramesh's feet and said, 'Please call me Rama.'

Ramesh felt as if someone had struck him with a whip. He stiffened and said, 'Very well, I was told that you were ill. So I wanted to know how you were now. Whatever may be your name, I've neither the desire, nor the necessity to call you by that name.'

Rama understood everything. She remained silent for a minute and then said slowly, 'I'm all right now.' Then she added, 'Perhaps you're surprised that I should've sent for you, but...?'

Before she could finish, Ramesh interrupted her and said sharply, 'No, I'm not. The days when I used to be surprised by your actions are long over. However, tell me why you've sent for me.'

Ramesh had no idea how cruel the blow was that his words inflicted on Rama's heart. She remained silent with downcast eyes for some time and then said, 'Ramesh-da, I've given you this trouble for two things. I'm fully conscious of my guilt for having caused you so much suffering. Yet I knew for certain that you'd surely come and that you'd accede to these last requests of mine.'

Her voice grew heavy with tears and she could not continue. It was so obvious that Ramesh noticed it and immediately all his old affections for her revived. He was himself surprised that his love for her had not died despite all the blows and counterblows and that it had only remained dormant in his heart all this time. He kept quiet for a while and then asked, 'What are your requests ?'

Rama raised her face for a moment and then lowered it immediately and said, 'The property which Dada is trying to seize with your help belongs to me – that is, you two have only one-sixteenth share in it and the rest is mine. I want to give it to you.'

Ramesh flared up. 'You needn't have any fear. I've never in the past helped anyone grab somebody else's property, nor shall I do so now. And if you propose to make a gift of it, you may give it to somebody else. I don't accept gifts from anyone.'

In the old days Rama would have immediately retorted, 'It's not an insult for a Ghoshal to accept a gift from a Mukharji.' But she did not say so today. Rather she said, humbly, 'I know, Ramesh-da, you won't help anybody grab anyone's property, and that even if you agree to take it, you won't use it for your own personal gain. But that's not it. One who does something wrong must suffer punishment. Why don't you accept it as a fine for all the wrongs I did to you?'

After a brief silence, Ramesh said, 'And your second request?'

'I'm putting Jatin in your hands,' said Rama. 'Please bring him up and make a man of him like yourself, so that when he grows up he can make sacrifices, smilingly, like you.'

All the severity in Ramesh's heart dissolved. Rama

wiped the tears from her eyes with the corner of her sari and said, 'I won't be here to see that. But I'm sure Jatin has in his blood the spirit of sacrifice of his ancestors. If he receives suitable training, one day he too may be able to hold his head high like you.'

Ramesh did not answer her immediately, but continued looking through the window at the moonlit sky. His heart had grown heavy with a profound sorrow such as he had never experienced before. After a long silence, Ramesh turned to Rama and said, 'Please don't involve me in all this. After a great deal of suffering I've at last been able to kindle a dim light somehow. I'm afraid it may be blown out by the slightest breeze.'

'You needn't be afraid any longer, Ramesh-da', said Rama. 'Your light'll never go out again. Aunty was saying that you had to face all the trouble because you took your seat on a high pedestal where the common man couldn't reach you. We pulled you down with the load of our misdeeds and put you in your rightful place. You've now taken your stand in our midst; that's why you're afraid. Such a fear wouldn't have arisen in your mind before. You were then beyond the village community... you're now one of its members. So your light'll never be dim again; rather it'll grow brighter day by day.'

The mention of Aunty's name excited Ramesh. He said, 'Are you sure, Rama, that the flame of my lamp won't go out again?'

'Oh, yes, I'm quite sure', said Rama firmly. 'I'm repeating the words of Aunty, who knows everything. This is your work. You must take charge of my Jatin, forgive me for all my sins, give me your blessing and bid me goodbye, so that I may go with peace in my mind.'

Ramesh's heart flashed again and again like a thundercloud. But he remained silent, with his head hanging down.

Rama added, 'I've one more request to make. Promise

you'll grant it.'

'What's that?' asked Ramesh in a low voice.

'You must never quarrel with Dada on my account?'

Ramesh was not able to follow her. 'What d'you mean?' he asked.

Rama said, 'If ever you come to know what I mean, remember how I endured everything silently and never made a single protest. When one day I felt that I couldn't tolerate it any longer, Aunty came and told me, "My child, if you go on stirring the lie, it'll have a fresh lease of life. It's a sin to prolong the life of a falsehood in one's impatience." I bore in mind this advice of hers and was able to overcome all my trials and tribulations. You too mustn't forget it, Ramesh-da.'

Ramesh looked into her face and kept quiet. Rama added after a pause, 'You mustn't feel sad that you can't forgive me today. I know for certain that what appears to be difficult to you today will become easy one day. I'm sure you'll then be able to forgive me with ease, for all my faults. So I'm no longer distressed about it. I'm going away tomorrow.'

'Tomorrow? Where're you going tomorrow?' asked Ramesh in surprise.

'Wherever Aunty takes me,' replied Rama.

'But from what I hear Aunty isn't coming back again!'

'Nor am I', said Rama, quietly. 'I'm taking leave of you forever.'

She lowered her head and touched the ground with it. Ramesh remained silent, absorbed in his thoughts. After a while, he got up, heaved a sigh and said, 'Well, go if you must. But won't you at least tell me why you're going away forever ?'

Rama gave no reply. Ramesh went on, 'Why you've decided to keep all your secrets to yourself and go away, you alone know. But I fervently pray to God that I may be able to forgive you one day with all my heart. God alone knows what torture it means to me if I can't forgive you.'

Tears streamed out of Rama's eyes and rolled down her cheeks, but Ramesh wasn't able to see that in dim light.

Rama again bowed to Ramesh silently from a little distance and the next moment Ramesh came out of that room. On his way home it seemed to him that his future and all his enthusiasm for work had turned hazy and unreal like the moonlight.

Next morning when Ramesh arrived at Bishweshwari's house she was launched on her journey and had taken her seat in the palanquin. Ramesh stood in front of the palanquin door and peeped in. 'For what fault of ours are you leaving us so soon, Aunty?' he asked in a voice laden with tears.

Bishweshwari stretched out her right hand and placed it on Ramesh's head. 'It's better not to raise the question of fault, my child', she said, 'because there's no end to it.' After a pause she added, 'If I die here, Beni will light my funeral pyre, in which case my soul will never attain salvation. I've had to pass this life burning in anguish! I'm running away in fear, Ramesh, lest I've to suffer in the same way in the life beyond.'

Ramesh was thunderstruck. From this one sentence, today he realized, as never before, the agonized heart of the mother. He was stunned for a while and then asked, 'Why is Rama going away, Aunty.'

Bishweshwari suppressed, with an effort, a very deep sigh. She then lowered her voice and said, 'There's no place for her in this world, my boy; so I'm taking her with me to put her at the feet of God. I'm not sure whether she'll survive her illness even there, but if she does, I'll ask her to spend the rest of her life in seeking the solution to a very difficult problem – why God had sent her to this world with so much beauty, so many virtues and such a great heart and then placed on her head such a heavy load of sufferings and finally cast her out of this world so ignominiously for no fault of hers? Was this done in pursuance of a meaningful and beneficent plan of His or was this just the play of whim of our society? Oh, Ramesh, there's none in this world so unhappy and miserable as Rama!' She couldn't say anything more; her voice broke. Nobody had seen her so greatly moved ever before.

Ramesh stood still like one dazed. After a little pause Bishweshwari added, 'I command you, Ramesh, never to misunderstand her. At the time of my departure, I don't like to blame anyone. But you must never for a moment disbelieve me when I say that you haven't got a greater well-wisher than Rama in this world.'

Ramesh started, 'But Aunty...'

Aunty interrupted him quickly and said, 'There's no "but" in this, Ramesh. Whatever you've heard is false, whatever you've learnt is wrong. But let this be the end of all your grievances. Let your work go on unhampered, gaining strength every day, ignoring all wrongs, hatred and malice – this is her last request to you. That's why Rama endured all the insults and humiliations, but never complained against anybody. She was dying a slow death, Ramesh, yet she never opened her mouth to complain.'

Ramesh remembered that Rama had told him something like this the previous night. He was overwhelmed with an uncontrollable outburst of tears which nearly choked him. Checking himself with all his strength, he spluttered out, with downcast eyes, 'Tell her, Aunty, her wishes will be fulfilled.'

He somehow managed to make an obeisance by taking the dust from her feet with his outstretched hand. He then rushed out.

GLOSSARY AND NOTES

Introduction

1. *Brahmin of the highest class:* The Bengali word is *kulin*. Rama, in the story, is born in a *kulin* Brahmin family, whereas Ramesh and Beni are not so, although they are Brahmins. *Kulin* Brahmins would sometimes refer to other Brahmins as 'low-caste'. (See also note 9)

2. *Landowner:* Zamindari is a system of land revenue collection introduced by the British, whereby large tracts of land comprising several villages became the property of *Zamindar* in lieu of payment of guaranteed land revenue to the government. The *Zamindars*, through their appointed officials, would collect rent from small landholders, and were effective rulers of the territory they possessed, although law and order were maintained by government officers. The *Zamindars* also often acted as the social, moral, and cultural leaders of the community. In the story, Ramesh, Beni, and Rama share a large landholding acquired by Rama's father.

Chapter 1

3. *Inner Courtyard:* In the old days upper-class conservative Hindus used to build their houses in two separate parts. The inner apartment was open only to the members of the family, their near

relations and close friends. The ladies of the family, who observed *purdah*, lived in the seclusion of the inner apartment and normally did not come to the outer apartment or appear before outsiders.

4. *Aunt :* Terms indicating family relationships in Bengal are somewhat more numerous than used abroad; for the all-embracing *uncle*, for example, any of the following relationships can be meant: father's younger brother, mother's brother, and father's sister's husband. In Bengali each relationship has a term attached to it. To make the story easily readable, I have mostly used the English terms of relationship, but I should explain that in the original novel the precise relationship has been shown.

Aunt : *Mashi*, mother's sister; even distantly related or unrelated. The spiteful lady, who lives with Rama, is her *mashi*, called *aunt* throughout. *Jyathaima*, father's elder brother's wife. In the story she is Bishweshwari, translated as *aunty* throughout. As with *mashi, Jyathaima* can refer to non-related women, if their status calls for it. *Dada-da*, elder brother, or one who is familiar enough to be addressed as such. Ramesh, being older than Rama, and a family acquaintance, is Ramesh-da. Beni is called Dada by Rama. *Didi-di*, elder sister. Contexts of use the same as *Dada-da*.

Khuro, Father's younger brother, or one who is treated (by virtue of living in the same village, being a friend, etc.) as such. Tarini Ghoshal, Ramesh's father, was the younger brother of Beni's father; he is referred to as Tarini-Khuro.

5. *Rama :* Pronounced Roma to rhyme with comma.
6. *Prayers :* The original Bengali word is *Ahnik* (same as Sandhya-Ahnik) — an obligatory daily

worship or prayer. A Hindu is required to say his prayers three times a day – in the morning, at midday, and in the evening.

7. *Funeral ceremony: Shraddha :* After a Hindu dies, his or her dead body is burnt to ashes at the cremation ground. The eldest son or the seniormost son present or the next of kin makes the ritual offering of fire to the body. After the usual period of mourning, the religious rites called *Shraddha* are performed by the sons for pacification and salvation of the departed soul. The ceremony includes ritual offering of *Pinda* – symbolic food or oblation – offered to the disembodied spirit of the dead. The feeding of Brahmins and offering gifts to them are essential part of the ceremony.

8. *Cremation fire lit by his son :* Among the Hindus where the dead are cremated it is customary that the funeral pyre should be lit by the eldest son; it is considered extreme ill-luck if this were to be otherwise. Here Ramesh, being away at the time of his father's death, could not light the funeral pyre.

9. *Kulin :* It is said that Ballal Sen, a king of Bengal who ruled in the twelfth century, first introduced the *kulin* system among the Brahmins. The title *kulin* was conferred on those Brahmin families who were noted for their caste purity and pious life. They were regarded as first in rank among the Brahmins.

In the course of time kulinism led to many abuses. As a *kulin's* daughter could marry only a *kulin*, eligible bridegrooms could not be arranged for many girls and they had to remain spinsters. Often a *kulin* Brahmin was tempted to marry, for the sake of dowry, a number of girls – sometimes a very large number. Such married girls used to

155

spend their lives in their parent's house and their husbands used to pay them a visit once in a while. This inevitably led to moral degradation.

10. *With unkempt hair, bare feet... :* During the period of mourning a Hindu has to observe a number of restrictions. He is forbidden to use the usual dress, bed, articles of toilet, etc., and from taking the normal food. He can take only boiled (not parboiled) rice and vegetables once in the midday and milk and fruits for the evening meal. He cannot use oil, shoes, or any clothes excepting a piece of dhoti and a *chadar,* i.e., a wrap. He cannot have a shave. He can sit only on a grass mat or on a woollen rug.

11. *Are you well? :* You is used in Bengali in two ways, equivalent to French *tu* and *vous.* The formal and respectful *vous* is used while addressing elders and unfamiliar persons. Close relatives and friends would use the equivalent of *tu.* Rama had addressed Ramesh with the formal *you,* although in childhood they used the informal *you.*

Chapter 2

12. *Vikrampur :* A group of villages in the district of Dacca (now in Bangladesh, previously in East Bengal and, after partition, in East Pakistan) is collectively known as Vikrampur.

13. *This part of Bengal :* Apparently West Bengal. From the reference in the text, such as the nearness of the village to Tarakeshwar and Balaram Mukharji's service under the Burdwan Estate, the setting of the story seems to be in the district of Hooghly in West Bengal. The author lived in a village in Hooghly district.

14. *Burdwan Raj:* Burdwan is the anglicized name of

Bardhaman, a town in West Bengal. Before the abolition of estates, the landowner of Burdwan was the premier zamindar in Bengal and had extensive estates in Bengal and Orissa. The title of Maharajadhiraj, i.e., the great king, was conferred on Sir Bijoychand Mahatab, a former zamindar of Burdwan, by the British Government.

15. *Servant of virtue :* Dharmadas explains his name. *Dharma* is virtue, right conduct, moral merit, das is servant; hence *servant of virtue.*

16. *House of worship : Chandi-mandap*: The building where Durga Puja (cf. no. 47 of the glossary) is held is called *Chandi-mandap* – the temple or pavilion of goddess Chandi or Durga. After the annual worship of Durga is over, the building is used for holding other religious festivals and also for miscellaneous purposes, such as musical soirees, recital of sacred books, etc. It is sometimes used as a club-house or a meeting place and sometimes the village *Tol* or Sanskrit school or the village *Pathshala* or primary school is held in this building.

17. *Consecration ceremony of a tree :* In the old days establishment of a temple, excavation of a tank for providing drinking water, and the planting of fruit trees, etc., were considered acts of piety. Consecration of a tree used to be solemnized as a religious ceremony.

Generally a group of five sacred trees – *Ashwattha* (Peepul), *Bat* (Banyan), *Bel* (Marmelos), *Amlaki* (Emblic myrobalan) and *Asoka* (Saraca Indica) with its deep red flower, collectively known as *Panchabati* – are consecrated and dedicated to the service of God. Many devout Hindus sit under their shade and offer prayers.

18. *Votive tray :* The original Bengali word is *Shidhe*. In all religious functions, a tray of basket contain-

ing eatables is offered as a part of the ceremony. It is taken by the priest or priests.

19. *Pouring ghee on burnt out fire :* When a *Yajna* (sacrificial rite) is performed, ghee is poured into the sacrificial fire as an oblation. After the *Yajna* is over, the fire is extinguished and no ghee is poured into it then. When someone does something which serves no useful purpose, this Bengali proverb is quoted to emphasize the utter uselessness of the action.

20. *Dhoti :* A piece of cloth, about 45" x 180", tied round the waist by men in eastern India, the common native Hindu dress; loin cloth worn as a lower garment.

21. *Luchi :* Circular (3" x 4" across), deep fried, rolled out discs of flour dough, considered a delicacy in Bengal.

22. *Sandesh :* A sweet made from cottage cheese kneaded with sugar boiled to a thick consistency; a popular Bengali delicacy.

23. *Ghee :* Clarified butter. A cooking medium in India. Expensive.

24. *Mihidana :* Fine globules of gram-flour fried and soaked in thick syrup.

25. *Rasogolla :* Ball of kneaded cottage cheese boiled in syrup.

26. *Khirmohan :* Flattened, oval, kneaded cottage cheese with condensed milk filling, boiled in syrup.

Chapter 3

27. *Woollen rug :* During the period of ritual mourning the orthodox Hindu practice forbids sitting on anything else.

28. *Goddess Lakshmi :* The goddess of wealth and happiness.

29. *Sudras* : The lowest caste among the Hindus; looked down upon by the higher castes, particularly in the villages.

Chapter 4

30. *Leaves were being laid* : In communal feasts, particularly in villages, people sit on the floor and eat off banana leaves or leaf-plates.
31. *Khanti Bamni* : Khanti, the Brahmin's wife. Khanti is a distortion of Khanto
32. *Koli:* According to Hindu scriptures there are four ages or time cycles, each one covering 432,000 years. *Koli* is the last, dominated by unrighteousness, untruth, pride, envy, and fear. The present cycle, *Koli,* began in 3101 B.C.

Chapter 5

33. *Annas* : Before decimalization, the Indian currency, rupee, used to be divided into sixteen annas, which were subdivided into four pice each. Each pice, again, was divided into three pies.
34. *Sacred thread* : A few strings of cotton thread worn across the body, from neck to waist, by Brahmins. A ceremony is held at around the age of twelve, after which a boy is considered to be twice-born and allowed to wear the sacred thread.
35. *Sacred thread wound around his ear* : Brahmins are required to tie the loose length of the thread around their ear while urinating or defecating, so that the thread does not come in contact with impurity.
36. *Grab my hands:* Utmost audacity; a fisherwoman is not supposed to touch a Brahmin.

37. *Taking the dust from his feet :* In Hindu society, younger people do this to older people and lower castes to the upper castes, particularly Brahmins, to show submission and humility.

Chapter 7

38. *Chhoto Babu :* Of the two Ghoshal landowners, Beni, being older is *Baro Babu*; Ramesh, being younger, is *Chhoto Babu*.

Chapter 8

39. *Goddess Shasthi :* Bestower of children and their protector.
40. *Dal and roti : Dal* is lentil soup, *roti* is flat unleavened bread; the staple food of northern India *(up-country food)*, unlike rice which is the staple food in eastern and southern India.

Chapter 9

41. *Chalta :* Name of a tree bearing a kind of sour fruit.

Chapter 10

42. *The life beyond :* The original Bengali word is *parakal*. Hindus believe in transmigration of soul and a cycle of rebirth until the attainment of salvation.
43. *Ritual sipping of water :* The original Bengali word is *gandush*. Brahmins are required to take a sip of water after chanting some sacred verses before any major meal.
Apparently the idea is to pacify the five vital airs in the nervous system of the body and to offer the

food first to God and then to take it as sanctified food.

Chapter 11

44. *Sacred basil plant :* *Tulsi* or the Indian basil is regarded by the Hindus as a sacred plant. They believe that *Vishnu* (the Lord of the Universe) is pleased when *Tulsi* leaves are offered to him during his worship. In fact, *Tulsi* leaves are used in all religious ceremonies and worship.
   In every orthodox Hindu home, there is a *Tulsi* plant in the courtyard, sometimes placed on a pedestal. Every evening the lady of the house places the first evening lamp at the foot of the *Tulsi* plant and makes an obeisance there, in the same way as before a deity.

Chapter 12

45. *Kayastha :* A sub-caste among Hindus.

Chapter 13

46. *Day of the ritual fast : Ekadashi* or the eleventh day of the lunar fortnight is observed by Hindu widows as a day of fast.

Chapter 14

47. *Durga Puja :* Worship of the Goddess Durga. This is the most important religious festival of the Bengali Hindus. It is held in autumn for five

consecutive days; out of which the principal ceremony is on the seventh, the eighth, and the ninth day of the bright fortnight. Immersion of the images in water takes place after the last day's worship.

According to the Hindu scriptures, when the demons defeated the gods and drove them away from the heaven, the Primordial Energy took the shape of a mother-goddess named *Chandi* or *Durga*. She killed the demons and restored the gods to heaven.

48. *Ceremony of feeding the first rice :* The original Bengali word is *annaprashan*. It is a religious ceremony for putting cooked rice into a child's mouth for the first time in his life, at a prescribed age. After this ceremony is over, the child is gradually introduced to food other than milk.

Chapter 15

49. *Sacred thread ceremony :* The original Bengali word is *upanayan*. When a Brahmin boy attains a certain prescribed age, he has to undergo a religious ceremony for his initiation into Brahminhood. He is invested with a sacred thread, which is the insignia of his Brahminhood. From the date of this ceremony, he has to say the obligatory prayers thrice a day, as prescribed for a Brahmin. Brahmin girls are not eligible for this initiation ceremony, nor are Brahmin women entitled to wear the sacred thread.

After this ceremony, one becomes a *dwija* (twice-born) – the second birth refers to the initiation into the mysteries of the Ultimate Reality.

Chapter 16

50. Consecrated food : Hindus offer sweets, fruits and also cooked food to a deity. They believe that the deity partakes of the food offered by a devotee, invisibly, in a godlike manner, though the quantity remains the same as before. The food so tasted by the deity becomes *prasad* or sanctified food or consecrated food.

Chapter 17

51. *Ayurvedic Doctor : Kaviraj* as he is called in Bengali; a practitioner of the ancient Hindu system of medicines derived from plants and minerals.

Chapter 18

52. *Benares :* Benares or Kashi is a famous place of pilgrimage for the Hindus and a famous centre of Brahminical learning. The temples of *Vishwanath* (the Lord of the Universe) and *Annapurna* (the mother-giver of all food) and the bathing ghats leading to the river Ganges are well known.
It is believed that those who die in Kashi go to heaven. Formerly many Bengali men and women used to go to Kashi and spend the last days of their life there.

Chapter 19

53. *Palanquin :* An oblong box-like structure, in which two or three persons could be seated, attached to a long pole, carried by two or more palanquin bearers.